Yvonne Coppard lives in Cambridgeshire with her husband and three children. She works as an advisory teacher (child protection), but has written several books for young adults, one of which was shortlisted for the 1990 FCBG Children's Book Award.

Other books by Yvonne Coppard

EVERYBODY ELSE DOES! WHY CAN'T I?

GREAT! YOU'VE JUST RUINED THE REST
OF MY LIFE

YVONNE COPPARD

Illustrated by Ros Asquith

PUFFIN BOOKS

For Ray

PUFFIN BOOKS

Published by the Penguin Group
Penguin Books Ltd, 27 Wrights Lane, London W8 5TZ, England
Penguin Books USA Inc., 375 Hudson Street, New York, New York 10014, USA
Penguin Books Australia Ltd, Ringwood, Victoria, Australia
Penguin Books Canada Ltd, 10 Alcorn Avenue, Toronto, Ontario, Canada M4V 3B2
Penguin Books (NZ) Ltd, 182–190 Wairau Road, Auckland 10, New Zealand

Penguin Books Ltd, Registered Offices: Harmondsworth, Middlesex, England

First published by Piccadilly Press, 1991
Published in Penguin Books 1993
Reissued in Puffin Books 1994
5 7 9 10 8 6 4

Text copyright © Yvonne Coppard, 1991
Illustrations copyright © Ros Asquith, 1991
All rights reserved

The moral right of the author has been asserted

Printed in England by Clays Ltd, St Ives plc

I hate my life. When I die, and I want it to be before I'm twenty-five, my tombstone will say: 'Her life was dull, but respectable'. Today I realized that it's all mapped out for me – hard work from the cradle to the grave, with nothing in between. I'm going to end up just like my mum – old and decrepit, with no memory of what it was like to be young and free.

I have the dullest parents of anyone I know. They think they're quite trendy (my dad even uses the word 'trendy'. Yuk.) When my friends come round, I just want to die when Dad decides to chat. Thank God he usually tells his one joke (it's so feeble it's not even worth writing down) and then goes back to his newspaper. As for Mum – well, she buys all her clothes at Marks and Spencer's. She also buys me things from there, and expects me to wear them. Enough said.

Today was a typical example of life with my parents. Just because I decided to go round to Sadie's tonight instead of working on my English assignment, I got the full works – 'irresponsible', 'devil-may-care attitude', etc. etc. What was I going to do when I reached the real world? Did I think GCSEs were going to fall out of the trees into my lap? etc. etc. There are a lot of etc.s in my diary – it means all the things they've said a hundred times before. You would think it was a crime to go out and see your friends a couple of times a week. There are other things in life besides GCSEs. I tried to point this out, but they weren't prepared to listen to reason. I made a dignified exit and left them to it.

15th October

Rotten day. I've got a stinking cold, and feel almost as old as Jenny thinks I am. There was a drunk in Casualty who wouldn't go away, and insisted on flashing his ankle at me. There was a bruise on it, apparently, though how he could see through all the dirt was beyond me. I kept telling him I was only the receptionist, but it was no use. In the end, a porter had to remove him bodily from the unit.

I really looked forward to the end of the shift and a quiet evening at home. No such luck. Mothers of teenage daughters give up all rights to peace and privacy. No sooner was I through the door than Jenny announced that she wouldn't be in for dinner – she was off with her friends. Mike pointed out that this was the fourth night running she's been out more or less straight from school. He wondered when she was planning to catch up with homework. Suddenly they were off, hammer and tongs, and I was in the middle of it all. I can never work out how that happens. In the end she stomped off anyway, and we were both too tired to stop her. Now Mike is looking all pinched and tense. It'll be ages before he gets to sleep.

A Girl's Guide to Parents

Lord & Lady Loadsaloot
(posh school and a BMW
when you hit seventeen)

The Winos:
Allow you **TOTAL FREEDOM**

Have you done your **homework**?
Tidied your **room**?
Fed the **cat/goldfish/terrapin**?
Written to **Grandma**?
Thanked Mrs Nice
for those lovely
headscarves?
No you **can't**
you're too
young. We're
not **made
of money**!
etc. etc. etc.
etc. etc. etc.
etc. etc.
etc. etc.

Twiggy Spring & Bud Young:
Really on your **wavelength**
(and not even married!)

Mr & Mrs Normal:
(Your parents and mine,
worse luck).

Another going-over from the parents about 'responsible attitudes' (in other words 'do more homework'). What have I done to deserve all this? I'm a reasonable, caring person. I like to have a good time, OK, but not if it harms anyone else. I'm kind to animals and I would even kiss a boy with acne rather than hurt his feelings. My reward for all this is to be shackled to a couple of old fogies who think that a wicked night out is a Chinese take-away and a bottle of wine in front of the telly . . . I know it's mean to go on about it – they can't help being old-fashioned, and they're doing their best. But it's so AGGRAVATING!

All this aggro with Mum and Dad has almost made me forget the BIG news of the day. There's a new boy at school. His name's David Slater, and he's been living in Australia for the past ten years, apparently. He is GORGEOUS – only capitals will do. He's very sporty, with lots of muscle and a great tan, too. He makes the other boys in the fourth year look like real wimps. And he has been put in my form! This has to give me a head start on the rest of the girls (who are already drooling at the mouth!)

Thank God for the weekend – a busy Casualty session and yet another tussle with Jenny have left me feeling like soggy toast.

Jenny really is impossible sometimes. I have to remind myself that underneath all that righteous indignation and contempt for everything we do and say beats the heart of our bright, sensitive, caring daughter. When the teenage years are over she will emerge triumphant. Until then we have to put up with a sulky little so-and-so who's got herself on to a roller coaster and decided to drag the family along for the ride. Roll on those freedom years when she will be off our hands.

Soon after Christmas I am going to be fifteen years old. You'd never know it if you talked to Mum and Dad. We've just had a big row about the party. They'll only let me have one if it's 'properly supervised'. I can imagine it; the tiny sandwiches and the lemonade punch, with the two of them hovering like hawks, ready to swoop whenever there appears to be a danger of lips making contact. Maybe they'll let us play musical chairs and pass the parcel. (That's after they've frisked everyone for drink on the way in, of course.)

Sometimes I wonder if they notice that I don't wear nappies any more. Jon is only six years old and he gets just as much freedom as I do. He is a particularly nauseating specimen of a little brother – all angelic blond hair and innocent round eyes while he stirs whatever trouble he can. Just because I was having a row with Mum and Dad today he sucked up to them something rotten. They don't even know he's toadying just to make me look worse. They think the sun shines out of his . . . .

I have decided not to say what I really think here because my English teacher says that you never know who will read your diary in future generations. I don't want my grandchildren to think I was a foul-mouthed old biddy. On the other hand, if you can't be really truthful in a diary, where can you be? So, let these things about Jennifer Anne Murray, be recorded for posterity.

I am hopelessly in love with David Slater, who doesn't know I exist and isn't likely to until the next century, when I might be allowed out from behind my textbooks.

I am dressed in a Marks and Spencer jumper bought by my mother.

I have a little poser for a brother and two ageing crocks for parents.

My social life is practically non-existent because for

the next two years I'm supposed to spend every waking moment improving my mind. (Who'll want it once it's improved? I'll never meet anyone to show it off to.)

That about sums up my life.

27th October

This diary is almost as much a record of Jenny's life as it is mine. She certainly seems to be running things sometimes. This month has been one long procession of rows, sulks and clever-clever remarks.

Tonight she wanted to discuss her birthday party. Since her birthday isn't until February, I asked – as politely as possible – whether we could get Christmas out of the way first. I was treated to a look of pure teenage disdain. Mike, of course, fell for the bait. He said of course she could have a party, but one of us would have to be there to keep an eye on things. Apparently Jenny would rather celebrate her birthday by shaving her head and splitting her throat. I was tempted to point out that the first is a bit of a wasted effort if you're planning to do the second, but I managed to bite it back.

Mike said she clearly didn't want a party after all, and she flounced up to her room in a sulk. Actually, this was quite a relief – at least she was out of the way.

Jon loves it when we're cross with Jenny. It gives him the chance to play the little angel-boy. He snuggles up for a cuddle, or offers to make a milk shake or fetch the newspaper. He is such a little poser. Still, it would be ungracious to let him know he's been twigged, and it's rather nice after a dust-up with Madam. So we lay back and let him wait on us a bit. Peace at last.

Today I went down to the Saturday market with Sadie. I bought this great skirt – black and floaty, almost to the ground. I think it's silk or something, and it's at least forty years old, the lady who was selling it said. Sadie found some black lacy gloves on another stall – the sort that don't have any fingers in them. Then we went back home and experimented with the make-up and stuff. Mum was down at the hospital as it's her turn to work the weekend shift, and Dad took Jon to the cubs' footer match, so we had the whole house to ourselves! I turned the stereo up loud enough to treat the neighbours to a bit of Proper Music for a change, instead of that boring classical stuff you can occasionally hear wafting out of their window. Then we raided Mum's make-up in case she had anything useful – it was good for a laugh, but nothing else! (I must have a talk with her some time to make sure she is buying stuff NOT tested on animals; in her day no-one worried about that kind of thing.)

I am getting a bit desperate for David Slater to notice me. I mean, he does smile at me now and then but he hasn't noticed me in *that* way. Rachel told me he goes to the sailing club after school, so I'm going to join. We can hoist the gib and splice the mainbrace – or whatever – as we sail into the sunset. That's plan A. Plan B is a change of image – the reason for the trip to the market. I was very tempted by some really cheap hair dye. I have always wanted to be blonde – sizzling white blonde, all shaggy and mysterious-looking. But apart from the fact that Mum would lay an egg if I tried it, Sadie pointed out that dye on top of perm would probably make it go green or something. So boring brown it has to be, at least until the perm grows out or I can afford a proper hairdresser. I can't risk doing something freaky. I'd stand no chance at all with David then.

The local hall has been booked for my party in March

– it's going to be a joint one with Polly Grant. (Her birthday's the day before mine). I went over to Polly's and we had a chat about strategy. We're saying nothing about the plan to 'supervise' us, but the battle has already begun. Polly and I are going to have a proper party (i.e., no parents) or bust.

7th November

Things seem to be getting better. Jenny hasn't been so sulky lately. I think she's looking forward to Christmas. She's also perked up enough to join the sailing club at school. I was surprised – she's never been very sporty, and hates the cold. But sailing seems to appeal – I hope it gives her something to channel her energies into rather than baiting her poor old parents.

Dad took Jon to a one-day cricket match (yuk!) so we had peace and quiet again today. Sadie brought a can of red hair spray that she had for her birthday, and we tried to get our hair to stand up in spikes. Sadie said she thought you had to stiffen it with sugar and soap, but we tried that and it didn't make our hair stiff, just mucky. We had more success with the eye pencils. After a few tries we looked really good. Noticeable, you know?

We're going to try it all out at the school disco at the end of term, so we need to practise! Until then we're keeping all the gear secret from everybody (especially our mums – even Sadie's mum would hit the roof if she saw us) and we're going to change at Cathy's on the way. Cathy is a real weirdo – she's got loads and loads of clothes, all the same: black and straight. Her mum's great – lets Cathy do almost anything she wants. She's a bit weird, too. She can't remember who we are sometimes, but she usually smiles and waves as we go upstairs, and she lets Cathy have friends round any time. My parents are OK most of the time, and I know I'm quite lucky in that. I just wish they weren't quite so dull.

We did have one disaster – well, two really. Sadie managed to get red hair spray on the bathroom wall, and I had to climb in the bath to get it off. I forgot to take my boots off, and they were a bit mucky. So we had to clean the bath – and the wall, because the bit I washed looked too obvious. Then the bath and one wall clean looked even stranger; we had to do the lot, so Mum wouldn't get suspicious. We both decided that cleaning bathrooms was not high on our list of fun things to do. It's hard work, and by tomorrow it'll be yucky again. Sadie says she is going to pay someone to do her cleaning when she has her own place. I don't know if I would be able to do that. It would be embarrassing – you'd have

to keep checking you hadn't left hairs round the plug and stuff like that.

Anyway, bath cleaning had its compensations. When Mum got home from work and saw the bathroom she thought we'd done it out of the goodness of our hearts, and gave us a pound each! I felt guilty about that later, so I played Lego with Jon AND gave him a bath AND a bedtime story while Mum and Dad had a quiet drink at the pub. I feel very noble now. And Jon is almost cute when he's scrubbed up (and asleep!)

8th November

It's been a long weekend. Yesterday was bad enough, but today Mavis was off sick, and I had to do double shift at the reception desk. Most of the people coming in were coughing and sneezing like nobody's business, as well as having the usual crop of broken bones and DIY wounds. Maybe we should run a 'flu clinic alongside the casualty department!

At least there was nothing too gory. Jenny thinks I am dealing with life and death all the time because she has seen 'Casualty' on the television. It's not usually that dramatic, of course. Usually I like weekends. Mike and I take the children out to a pub for lunch or something, and we're all home together. It's not often that we get such quality family time so it's a bit annoying when I have to work.

By the time I got home this afternoon I was tired and miserable, and just wanted a long hot soak before dinner. I was astonished, and very touched, to find that Jenny and her friend Sadie had cleaned the bathroom; not just a quick wipe-round either, but a really good job. Later, she even offered to look after Jon while Mike and I went out for a drink. It was a lovely surprise. I may have judged Sadie a bit harshly in the past (she has always seemed a bit sly to me) but I must admit now that she may be having a good influence on Jenny!

Preparations for Christmas are almost complete. I've just a few more presents to buy, and I promised to make the Christmas cake this year. We have arranged to go to my parents as usual – Devon is just the place to be for a real old-fashioned country Christmas. It will be lovely to roam around the beach with the kids, and play charades and so on instead of watching television all day.

27th November

The end of term seems like it's never going to come. Today Miss Bates gave me a long lecture about pulling my socks up and taking my work more seriously, yawn, yawn. I can't wait for Christmas, even if we do have to spend it buried in Devon with Grandma and Grandpa. I love them dearly and it's good to see them, but they live so quietly it's hard to keep awake! They even think telly is a bit wicked, and needs to be rationed so that the 'little ones' – that's Jon and me – aren't corrupted by it. Spending time with them makes you begin to see how Mum turned out the way she did.

I just interrupted this bit of writing to go to the bathroom and check on my spots. There are three: one really big one and two about to show up any minute, all clustered round my nose. I know I should be grateful I'm not smothered in acne (Hazel Beckett would never even be able to count *her* spots) but I'm desperate for a way to get rid of them. How can David Slater possibly like me, looking like this? (He, of course, has almost no spots at all.)

We had a bit of a shock today — a letter from Jenny's form tutor saying that Jenny is not making enough effort with her coursework. Her school report is not good — all the teachers say the same thing, which is that she doesn't seem to be taking things very seriously. Mike and I are very worried — we don't want her to blow her chances of good results next year. But she's been so much happier lately, and easier to get along with, that we don't much fancy having it out with her. She's really getting into sailing; it's so good to see her developing an interest.

Jenny's read the report, so she knows it's pretty bad, but she doesn't seem very worried. She doesn't know about the letter. We're going to have to crack down on her — but after Christmas. We'll have a good long talk, and a few New Year's resolutions.

Jon has finished his letter to Santa. It took a long time because it was a very long list. Most of the items are things I've never heard of. They must be space creatures of some sort. I have pointed out that Santa is not made of money, and other children will want things too, and he was very sweet about it. Santa can get as many things as he can afford, and that will be all right.

I have been sailing three times now, so I feel I have experienced enough of it to know my mind. I HATE IT! What a stupid way to spend your time – if I wanted to be cold and wet I could have more fun sitting in the bath fully-clothed. Of course, there wouldn't be the added pleasure of a force nine hurricane whipping through my clothes and messing my hair, or being bashed on the head with the boom when I don't duck quickly enough, but I could manage without them.

I'm not quitting, though. David Slater actually *spoke* to me today. He asked me if I needed help with the sail of my dinghy. He's a brilliant sailor (of course). He leaned really close while we were messing about with the sail, and smiled at me! If he likes the look of me in grotty anoraks and life-jackets, with hair like a haystack and no make-up, he'll go wild when he sees me done up at the disco!

As soon as we're going out together (only a matter of time, according to my horoscope) I'm going to ditch this sailing business. Honestly, the things we do for love.

I helped Jon with his letter to Santa. I tried to steer him towards stuff I know Mum and Dad can get. Last year he wanted a cuddly caterpillar – and they FOUND one! That was impressive, but they deserve a break, so I did my best to 'suggest' sensible things. At times he can be quite cute.

Only one more week of school – seems impossible I've survived, but here I am.

The school disco last night was FANTASTIC, once I got there. Nearly didn't make it – the parents tumbled that the skirt and T-shirt I had on was not what I was really going to wear. Mum spotted my bag. I had to show them the black stuff – thank God Sadie was looking after the belts and chains or I don't think they would have let me leave. As it was, there was a bit of fuss about me looking like a widow but then Mum acted like she was a real cool parent – said I didn't need to sneak out of the house and change somewhere else, I could have put the stuff on at home. If she could have seen me after we left Cathy's she would have laid an egg. Cathy lent me her make-up, and Sadie got our hair just right.

The old fogey at the door didn't want to let us in – he's somebody's parent. Almost makes mine look trendy. Half the teachers didn't recognize us, and half had a good laugh. Sadie was in a bit of a huff because they thought we were dressing up for a joke, but I told her that to be misunderstood by the likes of them was actually a compliment – who *wants* to be on the same wavelength as people who watch 'World in Action' and nearly wet themselves if they miss the nine o'clock news? She cheered up after that.

The best bit of all was that David Slater was really knocked out by the gear – asked how long the make-up had taken, and whether we went for that look all the time. I said only on special occasions, and he laughed. He said that was good, because he'd been planning to ask if I wanted to go sailing over the holiday, but he couldn't cope with me looking like that on a boat! Then he asked me for a DANCE!!!!

To be truthful, it was not all that romantic. It was a disco number rather than a smoochy, and we didn't actually touch. But with the music so loud we had to get quite close to shout in each other's ear! I was very hopeful, but he had to leave early for some reason (he did tell me but I couldn't hear what he was saying properly). Still, at least he didn't dance with anyone else. I'm in with a chance, surely (?)

He's got to go to his grandparents for Christmas, too. I just knew we would have a lot in common. Anyway, he's going to give me a call after Christmas to fix up some sailing. IS THIS A DATE?!

I was late back from the disco – it took me ages to get that stuff out of my hair. Mum talked about 'responsibility' and 'concern for others' as usual, but who cares? David Slater has noticed me!

13th December

Jenny gave us a good laugh last night. It was the school disco, and she and Sadie have been whispering in corners about it for weeks. Mike and I couldn't figure out what they were up to, and I was beginning to get quite worried about what they had planned.

When it was time for her to leave, Jenny came downstairs wearing a very ordinary – suspiciously ordinary – skirt and T-shirt. Clutched in her hand, half-hidden behind her back, was a bulging carrier bag. The way she edged towards the door, thinking she was being very cunning, was a hoot. I asked her what was in the bag and she went bright red. 'Just me boots,' she muttered. 'In case it rains.' Honestly, I could have fallen off my chair, but I kept a straight face and asked to see. Jenny's expression turned sour, and she half threw me the bag. Inside were some awful black rags (skirt, top and old man's waistcoat, by the look of it) and some lengths of tatty black lace. Underneath it all were the Doc Martin's we bought her for last year's walking holiday.

She was obviously intending to change somewhere else – Catherine's house would be my bet – and transform herself into one of those hideous Gothic creatures. Presumably Sadie or Catherine had the make-up and hair glue waiting. And here was I thinking all sorts of things – I even thought she might be planning to take drink or drugs. School discos in my day were dreadful for that sort of thing. To find out it was just a costume was quite a relief. Not that I told that to Jenny, of course. I acted surprised, and said if it was only black clothes she was trying to hide, it wasn't worth the bother. We don't mind what she wears, after all.

Jenny went off with a smug smile, thinking she had pulled one over on us, and Mike and I settled down to a quiet evening without her stereo blasting through the place. A good time had by all, I should say.

I think Jenny forgot about the time it would take to restore herself to 'normal' because she was half an hour late back, and even then she looked like a battered panda. I bet she must have been a sight in the full regalia. I wish I could have seen it. Anyway, I gave her the usual lecture about being late, but it was hard not to laugh.

19

Mike's just told me he has to go to Paris tomorrow. Some blasted computer has shut down at European HQ, and he's got to go and sort the system out, or something. I wasn't very good about it, partly because I was so exhausted from all the running round getting ready to leave for Devon. Now we can't go because Mike's not sure when he will be able to get back. I phoned Mum and Dad. They were upset, but very understanding. I don't want to go all that way without Mike to share the driving. He jollies Dad along, too, and it's a bit of a strain without him. So now I have to get a turkey and so on and prepare for Christmas at home. I know it's not Mike's fault, but I think I made it sound as though it was, and I feel awful now.

The children will be really disappointed not to have their traditional Christmas. Still, we'll have to make the best of it.

Great Christmas. We couldn't go to Exeter after all. Dad had to go off to some meeting in Paris. I got a new diary from Gran, and a voucher to buy some records. I also got some new jeans, a jumper and a make-up kit from Mum and Dad, a bar of chocolate from Jon (that's about as far as a six-year-old's imagination stretches, apparently!) and loads of other things.

Grandma and Grandpa sent me money, so did a couple of the old aunts and uncles. I've got forty pounds to spend after Christmas. I can hang around the market and choose some really good clothes. What Mum and Dad bought is all right (never look a gift horse in the mouth, and at least it wasn't a frock!) but they have a very *sensible* taste in clothes.

It was weird not being at Grandma's for Christmas. We've always gone down to Exeter ever since I can remember. Mum was really cheesed off about Dad going away. I expect she thought he would ooh la la with a mademoiselle de la nuit (my French is coming on nicely). Also, she likes the old log fire and country Christmas bit. But Mum is great at making the best of things (I suppose she has to be, with us daft lot to look after!). Actually, I'm glad we stayed home – it was a bit draggy being there year after year. Mum and Dad and Jon enjoy it but I'm a bit old for the silly games and stuff. This year was much nicer. We all pitched in and helped Mum with the Christmas dinner. I think it's important to show willing on special occasions. Mothers shouldn't be lumbered with all the work (especially as I will probably be one myself someday!)

I watched loads of telly and Mum didn't moan about it once. I met up with Sadie and Janice on Boxing Day, over at Sadie's. She got some great CDs for Christmas – her mum is a bit more in tune than mine. We compared presents, moaned about the old crocks, and worked our way through substantial quantities of shandy and crisps (and turkey sarnies, of course!) All in all, I had a great Christmas. AND David Slater AND my party still to come . . .

Christmas was not as disappointing as I expected, in the end. Mike managed to get back for Christmas Eve, and I had a long talk with Mum and Dad on the phone. They will come up here when the weather gets better, so we'll still see each other.

The children were very good about having their traditional Christmas torn away at such short notice. Jenny was actually kind, and said she was sad for me, but that she and Jonathan would manage.

It worked out reasonably well. I rather enjoyed being in charge of the Christmas dinner instead of being the assistant, even if I did feel frazzled by the time it was actually ready for the table. Jenny made a very noble speech to Jon and Mike about everybody having to pitch in and help, and then peeled two or three potatoes before waltzing off to do something more important (her hair, I think). She didn't reappear until two minutes before we ate, with a cheery 'Anything else I can help you with, Mum?' that almost drove me to throttling her. It's the thought that counts, I suppose.

Christmas afternoon fell a bit flat. I felt sorry for the children. We don't even have a chimney in this modern house, so the log fire was out, and there are no woods or beach nearby to go to after dinner, the way we usually do in Devon. Jon seemed happy enough, but I think Jenny was thoroughly bored. She sat slumped in front of the box most of Christmas Day, and went over to her friend's house on Boxing Day to escape the boredom here.

I have started the new diary Gran gave me a bit early, because the old one was nearly full and anyway, it seems a good idea to start on New Year's Eve, when you're looking back on the old year and planning the new. This is my second year of writing – I'm quite proud that I've kept it up. Mum says it's a journal, really, not a diary. In a journal you write as much as you like whenever you like. She has one, too. I wonder where she hides it; I've never seen her writing down her innermost secrets. I bet it's full of shopping lists and cake recipes. Nothing much happens to you once you're over thirty, so keeping a journal must be quite hard work. I'm always thinking of things to put in mine, but I forget most of them. Still, I've included it in my New Year resolutions – to faithfully write something every day (well, more often, anyway).

My other New Year resolution is to stop myself fancying David Slater because he fancies himself so much that there's not a lot of room left for a second admirer! He was supposed to call me when he got back from his gran's, but he didn't. Sadie says he came back two days ago – she saw him at the paper shop. So even if he calls now, it's not going to be the same. If he was really keen he'd have phoned earlier. If only he didn't have such a lovely smile, and such lovely dark eyes, and . . . here I go again. I think my only resolution ought to be never to make another New Year resolution – I could keep that one!

Well, I've written loads already, and not got around to any interesting news or intimate confessions (except that I really fancy David Slater, which doesn't count because I'm hoping it won't be true for very long). I'll have to save the rest for another time – my hand's about to drop off!

Off on the annual culture trip to London. Mum has this idea that it's important for Jon and me to spend hours in art galleries and museums and stuff – our national heritage, she calls it. Right flaming bore is more like the truth. I don't mind the museums at Kensington so much. We went to the Science Museum and the National History Museum last year – even Jon had a good time, and he's usually a real pain when you take him out anywhere. He whines like mad about being hungry, or tired, or thirsty. This year Mum decided that I needed (note the use of the word 'needed') to see 'our great art collections', and that Jon was a bit young. (In other words, she couldn't face him whinging on all day, either). So Jon went off to his friend's house for the day, to watch telly and eat sweets until Dad picked him up and took him to McDonald's – tough life for a kid, eh? Meanwhile, Mum and I went on this great 'treat' to London.

Only my mum could travel all the way to London in the middle of the sales to go to art galleries. I tried to edge her towards Oxford Circus – I had my Christmas money still to spend – but no, 'We can shop any time,' she said, and steamed off to the National Gallery. Feeling very noble, I didn't push the point. The poor old woman is trying her best, and it felt like I was sort of giving her an extra Christmas present, doing what she wanted to do. I didn't feel so noble after we'd traipsed round the fifty-ninth room of stuffy paintings, though. It took me about two minutes to whip round and look at the pictures – most of them looked pretty much the same. In every room I had to hang around waiting for Mum – she stood in front of each and every single painting as though she was reading a book. I was so bored my skull was caving in, but she had a good time. We had lunch at a little sandwich bar just off Trafalgar

Square, and then went in a taxi to the Tate Gallery, by the river. I felt really posh driving round in a taxi. The driver told me he'd driven all sorts of stars around in his time. He even drove Jason Donovan and Kylie Minogue to the Palladium once. Wow! Two or three years ago that would have really impressed me, but now it's only mildly interesting. I must be maturing. I asked if he had ever driven Patrick Swazey anywhere, and he said, 'Who?' Taxi drivers really ought to keep up with the times if they want to get swanky about hob-nobbing with the stars.

Anyway, I've written loads and loads and not got to the best bit yet. The Tate Gallery proved to be Very Interesting Indeed. Not the pictures and stuff – what a load of rubbish (literally – there were sculpture things made out of old tin cans and bottles, the sort of junk that Jon could make if he wanted to, but he's got better things to do with his time). No, there I was lurking about trying to look interested and wishing Mum would hurry up and then I saw this fantastic boy – David Slater is out of my life for ever. He was tall, and blond, but tanned, like he'd been on holiday. He was doing some kind of drawing in front of this great big painting that was all sorts of blobs and dots – I think it was a garden pond or something, but it was difficult to tell. Anyway, he looked up from his pad and smiled at me. My knees went all wobbly. I pretended to be really interested in this blobby painting, and sort of studied it as though I knew what it was about. But he didn't look up again. I went round the room slowly, staying by each painting for a long time so that he would know I was the arty type, and then went back to stand beside him. He looked up again and said, 'They're great, aren't they?' I said, 'Yeah, they really are, aren't they?' I was hoping he would show me what was on his pad, but he didn't. He just smiled again and went back to it. Ah well. He's probably a wimp anyway – but I would have liked the chance to find out!

Today I took Jenny to London. I usually take both children, but this time I decided to leave Jon with a friend. There won't be too many more years when Jenny and I can do this kind of thing together, and I thought she would really appreciate the time for just the two of us. We went to the National and the Tate galleries. It's the sort of trip that's good to do without Jon in tow. Painting and sculpture don't really figure in his world (except for posters and plastic space creatures wearing masks and carrying weapons).

I must admit I was tempted to skip the National and walk on down to Oxford Street. Jenny mentioned it first – she said she wouldn't mind if I would rather go shopping instead. That was very noble of her and I was quite touched, but I wanted her to see the originals of some of the paintings she has only ever seen on posters or cards until now. Actually I was a bit disappointed by her reaction. She thought the da Vinci cartoon was 'quite nice', the Rembrandt portraits were 'a bit yellow-looking' and the Turners 'washy'! I think she spent longer browsing round the gift shop than she did in the entire gallery.

Still, she seemed cheerful enough when we took a taxi to the Tate. Things lightened up there. Jenny was highly indignant about some of the modern sculpture. She insisted that even Jon could do better. I was embarrassed – she did not express her opinion very quietly, and a few people around us smiled. I didn't want to silence her – it's the beginning of a critical sense, even if the expression of it is a bit immature. But I wish she had a more positive attitude. Culture has to move on, explore new ideas, and Art is in the forefront of change, or it should be. I tried to explain this to Jenny, but she just said if that was what Art was going to be about, thank God she hadn't included it in her GCSE options. I got a bit annoyed then, but I managed to bite it back.

In the end, the trip did prove fruitful. Jenny discovered the Impressionists. She was very taken with Monet's 'The Lilies', and became quite absorbed in it – and in the other paintings around it, all impressionist. So my daughter is not going to be a philistine after all. Culture is at last beginning to make its mark. I must remember to buy her a book about Monet for her birthday. It has been a lovely day for us both.

Back to school today - what a drag. The old crocks gave me a real going over last night about homework – Attitude, New Term, Fresh Start etc. etc. Mum started out being all reasonable – she's obviously read that book Gran bought her for Christmas ('How to Handle Your Teenager'), because she was trying all the tips out on me. Trouble is, I've read it too, so I was ready for her. Then she reverted to type – 'Do as you're told and don't be so ****** cheeky.' I had to promise to be a good girl and do my homework straight after tea every night, just to stop the nagging. I get parole at weekends, but I have to stay home FOUR NIGHTS A WEEK! I just hope they're sorry when I have my nervous breakdown from overwork and imprisonment.

Today turned out to be OK, though. David was really sorry about not calling me. He'd lost my number and we're not in the book. He even wanted to ask Sadie my address when he saw her in the paper shop, but she left before he had a chance to speak to her. Typical of Sadie!

In history, we have to work in pairs on a local history project. David's got this really neat idea about tracing the history of some local people who got transported to Australia – his uncle is still out there and could give us a hand from the Australian end. Sounds impressive stuff – and he wants *me* to be his partner!

He's coming round tomorrow so we can go to the library and start our . . . research together. I haven't the foggiest what to wear – I want to look sort of serious, like a proper researcher, but devastatingly attractive as well, so that he HAS to ask me out for a Coke afterwards or something. I have to stop writing now – Sadie's coming round to look through my wardrobe with me and help me decide. Thank God I got some new make-up for Christmas.

If my little brother comes near me, I'm going to kill him. No, first I'll tear apart all his space creatures before his very eyes, *then* I'll kill him. He's probably ruined my chances with David for ever. I hate him – Jonathan, that is, not David.

Everything was going so well. We went to the library, found some good books to get us started and a couple of addresses to get more material from. I asked David in for coffee, and he said yes. Great. I took him into the dining room, so we could talk without Mum and Dad gawping at us. Fine. We chatted, and I could see I was really making an impression. He was asking me about going sailing, and he leaned over (close) to say something else. Suddenly there was this disgusting noise from behind the curtains, a sort of over-the-top raspberry. Jonathan! He'd been hiding there all the time. I was going to wallop him one, but I don't know David's views on violence so I decided against it.

David asked Jonathan what he was doing and Jonathan said he was waiting to see us kiss! I didn't know where to put myself, but there was worse to come. The little frog said *I* had said David must be a great kisser, and Jon just wanted to see if it was true. He must have been plastering his disgusting little ears to my bedroom door again, when Sadie and I were talking. David tried to laugh it off, but I could see he was embarrassed, and he left. I bet that's it for David and me. How am I going to face him tomorrow?

And what did my parents do when I told them? Fell off their chairs laughing, that's what. They didn't even tell Jon off, much less stop his pocket money or take away his latest Lego pieces which was what I suggested. So much for Supportive Parenthood!

31

We are in Jenny's bad books. We are Awful Parents, probably the Worst in the World; we have Failed our Only Daughter. Being in our house at the moment is like being on stage at some Victorian melodrama revival.

Yesterday Jenny came home full of excitement about a project she's doing for history. I was very heartened; it's the first sign of any enthusiasm for schoolwork, and I thought our talk a couple of days ago must have made an impression. I was very soon disillusioned when Jenny's project partner – a young man named David Slater – came to escort her to the library.

You don't need to be her mother to see that Jenny is potty about him. This seems very sudden to me, but I know how to count my blessings. In my day, to be seen with such a wholesome, clean-looking boy would have been the kiss of death. Boys your parents liked the look of were definitely out, black leather and long greasy hair were in.

Jenny brought her young man in for coffee. She was trying to look very assured and grown-up. She actually asked us if we wanted some coffee, as if she were in the habit of doing these small favours for her poor ageing relatives. Mike sniggered and I had to kick him quite painfully on the ankle. We behaved ourselves fairly well when Jenny suggested (oh, so casually) that they should discuss their project in the dining room so as not to disturb us. Jon, who had made an embarrassing start by asking David if he were Jenny's boyfriend (mercifully while she was out of the room) disappeared like a streak of lightning. I should have twigged what he was up to, but I was too busy watching Jenny's cool kid act to take much notice of Jonathan.

The next thing we knew there was this shriek of rage – not very cool – from the dining room and Jon was hauled in front of us like a common sheep stealer, with

demands for all sorts of punishment. He had been
'spying' on Jenny and David. Mike asked what they had
been doing that was worth spying on, but Jenny was in
no mood for humour. David made a fast, red-faced exit,
and Jenny gave us a thorough basting. The trouble was,
the more righteously indignant she got, the funnier it all
seemed. When she described Jon making a noise —
'blowing raspberries and pretend kisses from behind the
curtain, Mum!' it was the end. Mike and I just howled
with laughter; we couldn't stop ourselves.

I'm glad it's not Mother's Day for a while. I have a
feeling there'd be no bouquet!

Grandma and Grandpa Murray arrived today, for a fortnight. It's great when they come. Not only do they shower
us with money and little presents, they also give us a break
from Mum's eagle eye. She's so busy trying to prove she's
the perfect wife for their adored only son that she has no
time to pester Jon and me! Seriously, I think it's quite hard
for her when they come to stay. I know Gran gets on
Mum's nerves, and I can understand why. She sort of
watches, in a kind of disapproving way. Difficult to
explain, exactly. I try to help by diverting attention a bit.
Anyway, there's been no nagging about homework and I
expect to be able to get out at night a bit more while the
grandparents are here. And all I have to do in return is
answer questions about schoolwork and listen to Grandad going on about the government. He hates everything
they do and everything they say, it seems to me – but he
always votes for them because his family always has. And
they think *teenagers* don't make sense!

I can't wait for my birthday. Polly and I can have
twenty friends each. Polly worked on her parents, and
they finally said we could have it on our own if my
parents agreed, too. Well, they could hardly refuse once
Polly's lot had said yes, could they? So, they've actually
agreed to leave us to it and just come at the end to make
sure the clearing up is done properly! I can hardly
believe it. I expect they trust Polly to 'do the right thing'.
She's always been a bit of a goodie. We've also agreed
to have just Coke or fruit juice to drink. Who cares – the
main thing is I'm getting a proper party, with loud music
and no moaning about it.

Polly and I are busy making plans for food, decora-
tions, music etc. Our tastes are quite similar, which is a
relief. We used to be best friends until she went off to the
posh private school. Since then we haven't seen each
other much, but we still get on really well.

I picked up Mike's parents from the station straight from work. I hate doing that, because I don't have time to organize dinner properly. Mike always says to get fish and chips, but Emily thinks take-away food is a sign of incompetence, and she makes me feel nervous enough without starting out wrongly. She always seems to be watching me, somehow. She never says anything – in fact she often tells me how wonderful she thinks I am – but I can't shake off the feeling that I don't quite match up to expectations. I suppose it was inevitable, with Mike being an only child, that there should be some friction between us. It's always easier at their house, probably that shows the problem is mostly me.

Still, the children always enjoy having them here. They love to listen to their grandpa attacking the Prime Minister. I think he uses the government of the day to exercise his brain cells and sharpen his wit. Albert has no real political persuasions. He always votes the same way, no matter what. (Emily is worse – she studies the election hand-outs very carefully, and votes for the candidate with the nicest eyes!)

I hope it will work out all right. At least Emily is on hand to help with all the baking and preparation for Jenny's party next week. She is a brilliant cook (of course!) and we are hoping to fill the freezer and then have little left to do on the day. Polly's family are supplying the drinks and decorating the hall, Jenny and Polly are taking care of the entertainment (I gather that boils down to lots of records and a borrowed stereo that has very big speakers!) I still feel a bit nervous about agreeing to let them have no adults at the party, but it's only round the corner and this is such a quiet part of town I'm sure there'll be no trouble.

I am absolutely exhausted. I had a day off today, and Emily and I spent almost the entire time at the supermarket or in the kitchen. I never want to look at food again. Emily just doesn't know when to stop. She makes ME feel old. I wish we had booked twenty seats at the burger bar or something. I can't wait for it to be over.

The boy Jenny has her eye on was round again this evening – don't know why, but I hope it was to ask her out. He seems a nice lad.

David came round last night to bring some tapes for the party. Sadie had asked him if he had any good party ones, apparently. I think it might have been an excuse to come round, but he didn't ask me out. Mind you, that might be because I looked like the Thing from the Depths. I was deep-conditioning my hair; I whipped the towel off as soon as I knew who was at the door, but it was a bit of a mess. I also had my oldest jeans on, and a jumper Mum chose for me. Not exactly an invitation to romance! I wish I had known he was going to come round. I feel like I've missed an opportunity!

I can't work out whether David's interested, but shy, or just sees me as a friend. I suppose I could ask him out – Gran would have a fit at the idea, but it's supposed to be all right these days. Trouble is, I really haven't the guts to do it.

The stuff for the party is all going smoothly – only two days to go! Mum and Gran have spent ages in the kitchen and there's food all over the place. It all looks great. They looked worn out tonight, so Dad and I did a mammoth wash-up. Jon has made these weird paper things for me. They're gruesome, of course, but it's the thought that counts and they're his very best effort. I'm going to hang them from the ceiling and pass them off as the latest in extra-terrestrial party decs.

When I read the last two entries I can hardly believe I was so excited about the stupid party. It was a Complete Disaster. I'll never have a party again; it was the worst night of my life.

Everything started off OK. There was loads of food, and Polly's brother did the music. Most people came late, and it was a bit hard to get the dancing going, but by nine o'clock everything was getting together. Dad 'dropped by' and seemed pleased – he even stayed for a drink and tried to dance a bit (this was a very embarrassing experience but, mercifully, a short one!)

So there I was congratulating myself on how well we had done everything. Then Polly came up and asked if I knew two boys over in the corner. I didn't – I thought they were her friends. Turns out they were gatecrashers. We didn't know what to do. I wish we had spotted them before Dad left. They were drunk and were passing a bottle around. Vodka, I think. I asked them to go, but they said Carly had invited them. Carly wasn't even there, so I couldn't check whether she knew them. (I asked her this morning and she said they'd heard her talking about the party and she'd told them they couldn't go!)

As well as all this, the party sort of divided into two. The kids from Polly's school said my friends were calling them snobs, and lacing their drinks with salt. But the kids from my school said Polly's friends were making jokes about Bradman Comprehensive being the dumping ground for brainless oiks. There was this awful atmosphere, with her lot dancing up one end of the hall and mine at the other. Polly said we should just ignore it and turn the music up, so I did.

It was OK for a while. Then suddenly there was a fight. One of the gatecrashers went mad (he was really drunk). He started hitting everyone he could reach, and then it seemed like everyone was fighting. I was terrified. One of Polly's friends fell against a window, and put her arm through it. There was blood everywhere.

Polly ran to the phone box to get an ambulance and I went to get Dad – there was nothing else I could do. He and Grandma and Grandad came back to the hall. They were great. The sight of all the blood had stopped the fights, but there was a lot of shouting and panic. Grandad simply bellowed at everyone (he used to be a headmaster!) and they froze. Dad gave out orders – the place was cleared, the floor was swept and someone washed the bloody bits. Polly's friend went off to hospital with Grandma.

Dad talked to the caretaker about the accident, and everything was sorted out. I felt dreadful when we got home. Dad looked awful. But he didn't shout at me or anything. He gave me a hug and said he was sorry it had ended like that. Mum even said it wasn't my fault – she and Dad should never have agreed to let us have it unsupervised. That made me feel even worse because I know they only gave in to make my birthday special.

I hope Polly's friend is all right; there was so much going on I didn't take in what was happening, but it looked serious. If she's badly hurt, it will be all my fault. Me and my stupid, stupid, independence.

Well, at least I've learned from what's happened. I won't be so pig-headed again. My parents are the best there are, I reckon. They really stood by me. Mind you, Grandma and Grandad had plenty to say. I expect to be lectured at least twice a day until they leave.

It's going to be awful at school tomorrow. I expect everyone'll blame me for not keeping things under control, but how could I? I wish I knew what David thought about it. I made myself look a real fool in front of him. It would almost be better not to see him at all tomorrow, but not seeing him would make me just as miserable. I can't win.

I didn't get round to writing anything last night because I was shattered after Jenny's party. It went badly wrong – there was a fight, and a girl was pushed through a window. Mercifully she's all right – bruising and a gash that needed thirteen stitches – but she nearly severed a tendon, which would have meant the loss of use in her hand.

At least Jenny had the sense to run home for help before the situation got completely out of control. Mike and Albert and Emily charged off, leaving me feeling helpless. Jon was in bed, and I couldn't leave him. They sorted everybody out. Albert and Emily looked as though they enjoyed the drama of it all, but I thought Mike was going to have a heart attack or something. Jenny looked pretty bad, too, very subdued and tearful.

We were stupid to let a bunch of fifteen-year-olds run their own party. We put our trust in Jenny – and rightly, because beneath all the teenage hype she's very sensible and caring. But it was unfair to expect her to control a large group of kids who don't all share her values. We were falling over backwards to try and be liberal, caring parents, and give her a birthday to remember. We certainly got that last bit right – none of us will forget last night in a hurry. Poor Jenny – I hope she doesn't go on feeling it's all her fault. If anyone is to blame, it's us and the Grants, the would-be trendy parents. Never again!

Polly's friend had to have thirteen stitches in her arm, but she's OK. I still feel dreadful about the party. I'm going to be a model daughter and pupil to make it up to Mum and Dad. They were great.

So, the party was a nightmare. But they say every cloud has a silver lining, and they're right. The party was the talk of the year at school, as I had expected. But no one blamed me – a lot of people came and asked if I was all right, it must have been terrible for me, etc. etc. One of the Sixth Form boys even came and asked me if it was true the police were called to my party – he looked really impressed when I said yes!

Just after lunch, David came up to me in the hall and asked if I was OK. He was really worried about me last night! AND he's finally asked me out – we're going roller skating on Saturday! Lucky I've still got some Christmas money left – I'll have to buy something to wear. There are no words to describe how great I feel, so I'm not even going to try.

26th February

The last couple of days have been very trying. Emily gave Mike a good talking to after the party, saying he should never have agreed to it in the first place, what was he thinking of, and so on. She meant me too, of course, but wouldn't come out and say anything to me direct. Mike and I already feel bad about it, so there was no need for the extra misery being heaped on. I'm looking forward to tomorrow – they're going home! I lay awake last night thinking about the girl who was injured – what if she had lost the use of the arm, or been even more seriously hurt? It makes me go cold all over just thinking about it.

Jon has been a real sweetie. He can sense that things are tense, and he keeps Grandma and Grandad occupied with little-boy chat and cuddles, which eases things a bit. Jenny is doing her best to stay out of trouble, and even washed up tonight without being asked. She seems to have bounced back from the experience, maybe because the Slater boy finally got up enough courage to ask her out (first proper date) on Saturday.

Tonight was THE night – my first date with David. I worried about it all day: what to wear, whether I'd kiss properly (or worse, not get the chance!) etc. etc. Kissing was the worst thing to think about. It's supposed to come naturally, everyone says – but what if it doesn't? What if you dribble, or bash his nose – or even worse, LAUGH? (I always giggle when I'm nervous.) I looked through all the mags I had, but couldn't find any articles about kissing. I wished I had time to write to 'Dear Annabel', because I always trust her advice, but I knew even if she wrote back before the answer was printed in the magazine, there wouldn't be time.

Clothes were yet another problem – he's seen most of my decent stuff and although I trudged into town I couldn't find anything I felt really good in. Help! In the end I wore my new jeans and a not-too-old blue sweatshirt. I needn't have worried – he was wearing jeans and a sweatshirt too. We have so much in common.

The whole thing was great. I can't think of words to describe it properly. We skated with our arms round each other, and when we kissed it was so natural. We didn't clink teeth or bash noses or do any of the things I was worried about. All those days at sailing club were worth it. David said he really likes me – he wants to see me tomorrow! We're just going for a walk or something. I can't wait to see him again! Does this mean it's the Real Thing?!!

The whole night was perfect except for one small thing – that small thing being the toad, Jonathan. When David came round he sniggered and kept making stupid jokes about David being my boyfriend. I could have killed him. But David took no notice, thank goodness. Tomorrow we're going to meet at the park (Jon's NOT coming!).

Going back to school was not as hard as usual after the weekend because I knew Dave would be waiting for me. Yesterday we went for a really long walk in the woods. All that stuff about boys only being after one thing is a load of rubbish. I think Dave was as nervous about kissing as me! But it was great. We just walked hand in hand – there was even a beautiful sunset as we walked home. Sadie would put her finger down her throat if she read this, but she doesn't understand. Maybe one day it will happen for her too. Dave is so sweet. He's everything I want. When I'm with him I feel as though nothing can harm me, and nothing can go wrong for me. He makes me feel important because he listens to me and takes what I say seriously. We've talked about almost everything already, and we agree on all sorts of things like politics, religion, clothes, music – everything, really. And the kissing is great, too!

It's hard to think about anything else, but I still have loads of homework to do. We're not going to see each other during the week, except at school. Dave has to work quite hard. He went to an English school in Aussie, but he still has gaps in his coursework because the courses were different. I hope it works out for us, being at school together. I think it will.

Can't think of anything else to write. Every thought, every minute, is full of Dave. What more can I say?

Jenny is floating round the house on cloud nine. David Slater took her out on Saturday, and they spent most of yesterday together too. They look so sweet together – and nervous. I have the feeling that David Slater is as new as Jenny to the dating game. He seems quite shy,

and a bit in awe of Jenny. When she's in full flow she can be a bit much – I hope she gives him time to breathe!

Personally, I am very grateful to the boy for taking our daughter off our hands for a few hours. Although she is more cheerful generally than she has been for a while, for some reason she and Jon are falling out in a big way. He teases her about David, as you'd expect from a boy his age. But Jenny's reaction is way over the top. That sparks Jon off even more, and they bicker and shout and complain all the time. I feel like knocking their heads together. Sometimes I long for the days when it was just Mike and me, pleasing ourselves. I love the kids so much, but now and then they make me long for escape.

Now that Jenny is launched on the Romance scene, it feels as though she is on her way out of the nest. Part of me feels really excited for her and part wants to hold on to her. And yet, just to come full circle, I like the time I have to myself when she's out with her friends and Jon's in bed. I feel as confused and mixed up as I sound. Being a mother is not always the lovely cosy occupation the ads would have us believe!

My assessment report came home today. It was much better. The parents crowed like roosters. They reckon it's all down to them making me stay in, and checking my work and stuff. Actually they're mostly right. It feels really good to get a nice report for a change. And I do know the assessments are important, because we don't have exams in the Fourth Year and the assessments become the end-of-year grade. It would be nice to face the mocks in December with some really good course-work and a vote of confidence from the teachers in their assessments. So all in all I'm quite grateful for having the whip cracked now and then. Not that I would admit any of that to THEM of course. Besides, part of the good influence has been Dave. He's always telling me to get homework out of the way first, and then you have more fun because it's not hanging over you.

We're together all the time now, except for football practice and things like that. Some of our friends make jokes, but we don't care. We want to be together. Dave makes me laugh – he's very witty. It's quite hard thinking up things to say back sometimes, but when I do he laughs as though they're really funny. We have the same sense of humour. He's teaching me to be less picky about food too. In Australia he ate loads of raw veg-etables ('veggies') and now he's hooked me on things like raw mushrooms and carrots and green peppers. So he's even good for my health, not to mention my skin. I haven't got a single spot at the moment (well, not highly noticeable ones anyway).

Being away from Dave is miserable. I even miss him between coming home from school and going to school the next day. It sounds stupid, writing it down, but I do. I think I'm in love. Sadie thinks I'm 'in love with the idea of love' (I bet she got that from a magazine!)

I am thinking about having my hair cut really short to

get rid of the perm and start again. I fancy something very short and spiky, but I suppose it's not just up to me any more. I'll have to ask Dave what he thinks – can't risk losing him because he's ashamed to be seen with me!

Jenny's school report made today a lot brighter. At last she seems to have knuckled down. There's still room for improvement but she's making the effort, the teachers say. Mike and I are so pleased – all that nagging seems to have paid off. I think Jenny's pleased too, but try getting her to admit that!

The romance is going well, judging by the semi-permanent grin on Jenny's face. She doesn't say much, but when she does it's straight out of a soppy comic.

Strangely enough, I think Jon is the one who has the hardest time with this new phase of Jenny's life. They were never terribly close, but Jenny would usually spend a bit of time with him at the weekends. Now David has put his nose out of joint: if Jenny isn't busy with homework, she's out with David. Jon tries to fight back by saying silly things about the pair of them. I think he's just covering up the hurt he feels at being left out. Mike and I are keeping our heads down, hoping they'll sort themselves out. I hope that's wise.

If there was a prize for the worst little brother in the world, Jonathan would win it, no contest. When I think that I was actually HAPPY when he was born, I could vomit. I thought I'd get this cute little brother to take to the park and buy sweets for. Yuk! Did I learn fast!

Not content with being his usual pest-like self, the little toad thinks seeing me and Dave together is the biggest amusement since Blackpool. He keeps asking Dave if he's in love with me. He makes kissing noises when he sees us together. I could die of embarrassment (he'd probably find that really amusing, too).

Yesterday I just couldn't take any more. I told him he'd better stop, or he'd be sorry. Today Dave came round to give me a book – and Jon started again. So I've hidden his Lego – the whole box, every single brick. He's not getting it back until he promises to leave us alone. Not even Mum and Dad know where it is, and I'm not going to give in. It's about time the little brat was made to behave. Since Mum and Dad can't control him, it's up to me.

Well, Jon promised he would be good, and it lasted for about half an hour. Dave came round, and Jon just couldn't resist having another go. Then he had the cheek to tell Dave I had stolen his Lego and wouldn't give it back. I told Dave the truth, but he doesn't have any kids in his family and I don't think he understands what it's like. When Jon gave his quivering bottom lip act Dave actually looked sorry for him!

Jon put on the pitiful sobs routine when Dave left. Dad yelled at me to give the Lego back. I did – I emptied it out of the bedroom window, all over the garden. It was sort of raining Lego bricks all over the lawn.

Jon started crying for real then. He was sobbing like he was heartbroken. I knew I'd gone too far that time. It was awful. I really wanted to back down, and say I was sorry. I even wanted to give him a hug. But I just couldn't. It was like I'd swallowed a stone. I could feel my face sort of setting, like cement. I just stood there and said nothing, while Jon sobbed and Mum and Dad got ready for a war dance.

Jon's still a spoilt brat, but he didn't deserve what I did to his beloved Lego. Mum and Dad are still furious and Jon sort of quivers when he looks at me, like I'm the Wicked Witch of the West. (That's pretty close to how I feel about myself, too.) I'm going to buy him some really nice Lego as soon as I've got the money.

Mum says Jon's being so awful because he's jealous of Dave. It's true that I'm wrapped up in Dave – who can blame me? But I guess it's a bit tough on Jon. He must feel left out. I can't say I've ever been a doting sister, but I suppose I do usually spend more time playing with him than I have done lately. I must try to keep a bit of my life free from Dave. But I just love him so much . . .

The Jenny v Jon saga came to a head tonight. Apparently yesterday Jenny took away Jon's beloved Lego box, and said she wouldn't give it back until he promised to leave her and David alone. Usually Jon would come running straight to me, but he didn't tell this time. Whether this was because he felt what he had done was naughty, or Jenny frightened him into believing she really would destroy his Lego I don't know. I don't like to think that she might have bullied him.

Jon promised, of course. He hardly knows what a promise means. Jenny said she would let him have the Lego back if he was 'good' all the time David was here today. Poor little boy – he loves that blasted Lego so much, I'm sure he tried. But all the jealousy and longing proved a bit much, and he started teasing them again. Jenny said nothing until David had gone, and then suddenly she turned to Jon and said, 'That's your Lego gone, then.'

Jon started to cry. I honestly don't believe he understood what he had done to deserve such a terrible punishment. I tried to explain this to Jenny, but Mike was so angry I hardly got a chance to speak. He told Jenny to give the Lego back straight away. He called her a bullying thug.

Jenny immediately stormed up the stairs and tossed the Lego out of the bedroom window! Jon's cries were pitiful. It wasn't temper; he was really upset. I suppose he thought the Lego would be smashed; maybe he even thought plastic bricks could feel pain. They get such funny ideas at that age.

Jenny helped pick them up, but she didn't seem exactly contrite. She thinks she was justified, and that we're spoiling Jon and favouring him against her. How can there be such a gulf of misunderstanding in one small family?

I'm sure we will all look back on this one day and laugh. It's one of those silly incidents that builds from nothing and suddenly explodes. You look back in later years and wonder what all the fuss was about.

I have finally got something to write about, after days and days of 'nothing much happened'. (Why is the world so boring? If these are the best days of my life, God help me when I get to the rest of them.)

Anyway, I actually enjoyed myself at school today. Yes, ENJOYED. Not a word I get to use too often about school. But today was fun.

Firstly, Sadie and I pulled a really ace April Fool stunt. We clingfilmed one of the loos in the girls' toilets (Dave kept watch outside). Who should be the next girl to come along and use it but (oh joy of joys) Helena Clondyke-Smith, Queen of Snobs, Miss Stuck-up herself!

There was this shriek from the cubicle, then dead silence. A couple of minutes later, she came out with a bright red face. Sadie and I were doing our hair. I pretended to be dead concerned, and asked if she was all right. She looked suspicious, but I've been practising this really innocent look, and the work paid off. She said, 'I'm fine, Jennifer, thank you.' Then she sort of swept out of the loo trying to look dignified. Sadie and I were falling about. I don't know how we made it to Maths.

Then Dave took a message to Miss Perks (Latin) that there had been a room change, and we were going to be in Room 32. Since Miss Perks gave up on life when the Roman Empire collapsed, she had no idea it was April Fools' day, and lugged herself up the three flights of stairs (no mean feat, if you saw her) to Room 32 only to find a note saying we were, after all, in Room 14 (ground floor). Actually, I felt a bit bad when she came puffing in, rosy pink and sort of crumpled all over. Still, she recovered. I suppose teaching something as crushingly useless to society as Latin must give you a pretty tough skin.

I can't believe it – two interesting days in a row! When I got home from school, there was a letter from my cousin Eleanor. She's getting married – and asking me to be a bridesmaid! Her fiancé, Greg, is gorgeous. They both work for the BBC. Eleanor is a production assistant (whatever that is) and Greg is a designer. He makes sets for Shakespeare plays and stuff, but you'd never know to look at him. They're both yuppies, but nice ones. They'll look fantastic at the wedding.

I always wanted to be a bridesmaid. I would have enjoyed it much more when I was five or six, but at least it will be a classy wedding. Eleanor has great taste in clothes. I can't wait to tell Sadie tomorrow. She'll be as green as old school dinners.

P.S. Talking of school dinners reminds me – they've asked Mum to make the cake! Brave decision!

We had a letter from Eleanor this morning. She's finally going to marry Greg and settle down. I am so happy for my sister. She was beginning to think she would never get to be a grandmother, with Eleanor being the only child. She says getting married must mean they're thinking about a family, and I'm inclined to agree. The fact that they are getting married in only three months time is pretty convincing!

Eleanor has asked Jenny to be a bridesmaid. Jenny tried to be casual about it, but I could see she was excited. I must say, it will be lovely to see her in a dress for once.

Susan wants me to do the cake. She said they wanted the cake to be made by someone who would make it with love. I feel quite touched. I've only just got to 'celebration cakes' in my evening class, but I'm sure the teacher will help out.

Apparently, they're going to go for the full traditional wedding. Eleanor wants a 'Fifties' theme because it was on a series set in the Fifties that she and Greg met – very romantic. They've designed the whole thing together, and friends in the costume department are pulling out all the stops to get them finished. Susan sounds quite excited, but she wouldn't tell me much. She says she wants to wait until we go up there to discuss everything properly. All I could get out of her (and then only by being sworn to secrecy) is that Eleanor's dress will be white crushed velvet, with a full-length veil and train, and the bridesmaids (Jenny, Greg's sister, and two nieces) will be in salmon pink satin. I hope Jenny's hair is long enough for the occasion. With Eleanor's eye for detail, if Jenny's hair won't go into a bouffant or beehive, or one of those Fifties hairstyles, she might have to wear a wig!

We're travelling up to spend the weekend with them all next month, and get all the details. There hasn't been a wedding in this family since Mike and I got married. I feel quite excited.

End of term at last! Two whole weeks and a couple of days – FREEDOM!! Usually the teachers pile on the homework so there's no chance of enjoying it, but someone's slipped up somewhere – we haven't got much homework at all!

Dave took me out to celebrate last night. We went roller skating and then to the burger bar. We walked in the moonlight up to Hunter's Hill – dead romantic! We're going to be together almost every day in the holidays!

It's hard to believe we've only been going out for a few weeks. It feels like we've always been together. I think I'm properly in love; not just kid's stuff, but the real thing. I know it can happen this way sometimes, that you know right from the start.

I think Dave is ready for a bit more than kissing. Sometimes I want to go further too, but something always stops me. Dave never pushes things, but I wonder if he's getting fed up. Sadie says all boys want to go the whole way, it's part of their manhood. But I don't feel ready for all that yet. It would be hard to say no, but I hope Dave would rather wait until it can be something a bit more special than a quick grope in the dark. That's what I like to think. Maybe I'm just scared? Scared of getting pregnant, scared of Mum finding out, scared that he'll drop me as soon as I give in, scared of AIDS and stuff like that.

Maybe I'm just scared of doing it. Maybe I'm frigid. But when I try to work out how I really feel, it's like my brain just goes round in circles. I get so confused. I suppose I'll just have to wait and see what happens.

End of school term for the children, and beginning of an exhausting fortnight for me. Mike usually takes a week off over Easter, but there's so much going on at work at the moment it looks as though he will be lucky to have a long weekend.

I'm not looking forward to this holiday. Usually it's quite nice. Jenny looks after Jon while I'm at work, and is even pleasant to him. This holiday she has lined up almost every day with David, and Jon will have to tag along during the morning. It's bound to lead to friction. The poor little boy feels so shoved out. I'll have to have a word with Jenny about giving him a bit of attention, and make sure that we go out together after work. Jenny has been a lot better since the Lego incident, but she's so wrapped up in her own love life she hardly notices anyone or anything else.

This boy of Jenny's seems a nice enough lad, but to hear her talk about him (which she does incessantly) you'd expect to strip off his shirt and find a Superman costume beneath. He can do no wrong. I suppose that's a natural part of first love (I honestly cannot remember!) but I hope she begins to see him as a human being soon, before she risks being hurt.

Back to school tomorrow. The holiday has just flown by. Dave and I have been everywhere: cinema, walking, swimming, skating, round to friends' houses – we even studied together. Dave is good at EVERYTHING. He's great at swimming and skating, he's in the school team for football and played cricket for a flash-sounding team in Australia. Apart from that he has an incredible memory for things like history and geography (things I'm hopeless at) and he can even spell brilliantly. All this would make you sick if he wasn't so lovely with it – and modest, too. He doesn't act like he knows it all, he just helps you out when you want it. He helped me understand lots of things I thought were just boring facts before. He's so clever, and great at making things seem clear.

Last night we even talked about sex and marriage and all that, and he told me that he would never force anyone into that sort of relationship. I think he sensed I was a bit nervous, and he was trying to let me know that he's not the immature kind who wants to keep score of how many girls he can have it off with. He's so considerate.

21st April

Thank God the kids are back at school tomorrow. This last fortnight has been awful. Mike has looked like a washed-out rag, and falls asleep straight after dinner. I've been dashing home from work to relieve Jenny from babysitting and then taken Jon out somewhere different every afternoon to try and cheer the woebegone expression off his face. The house is a mess and the ironing has the shape of an enormous breeding monster about to take over the dining room. I asked Jenny to give Jon a bit of attention, but it seems she interpreted that in terms of treats like going to the park – she takes him to the park and then she and Dave sit on a bench absolutely absorbed in each other while Jon plays on his own! I was just too exhausted to push it any further; after all, she does look after him without complaining. That's more than some teenagers would do.

Jenny is the only cheerful one in the family at the moment. The old saying 'Love is blind' has taken on a whole new meaning – we're on the point of collapse and she hasn't even noticed! Mike and I have rotten colds and are exhausted and Jon is lonely, and fed up with his sister's love-life. Meanwhile, Jenny floats around on her own little cloud. Ah to be young again!

Sadie phoned tonight – Pete Kelly asked her out! She's fancied him for ages. I'm really pleased for her. Pete and Dave are good friends too, so we'll go out in a foursome.

Dave's got a job in the burger bar on Sunday and Thursday nights, starting next week. I didn't even know he was looking for a job, never mind planning to throw away our Sundays together. I was rotten to him but we made up. He needs the money because he's saving for a bike when he's old enough – just a 125 cc but enough for us both to go out on. We still have Friday and Saturday nights, and we can do homework and stuff together. I'm trying to be very understanding, but Sunday nights will be very lonely now. He doesn't even want me to come to the burger bar while he's working – says it will be a distraction!

First Sunday night without Dave. Sadie was out with Pete, so I went round to Cathy's. Her mum was out, and we watched telly, played records and talked. Cathy has problems with her mum. She told me she gets drunk a lot, and forgets to buy food. Cathy ought to try life at *my* old place. OK, I get fed but I'd sooner look after myself than have the great inquisition *every* time I want to go out. Cathy can go where she likes, when she likes. She doesn't know how lucky she is.

The evening was all right, but I missed Dave. We're not seeing each other (except school) until Wednesday — *and* I'll be away all weekend at Aunty Susan's, discussing the wedding. Life's cruel.

Just got back from Aunty Susan's. I can't believe what they're trying to do to me. Eleanor wants her wedding set in the dark ages. She actually thinks I will wear this DISGUSTING dress that even Helena Clondyke-Smith wouldn't be seen dead in. It's gruesome shiny material in a REVOLTING pink. I hope they're not having salmon vol-au-vents at the reception – no one will be able to tell us apart!

Eleanor also thinks I'm going to have my hair made into a sort of bird nest – she even talked about straightening my perm out! I feel completely betrayed. I thought Eleanor was really modern. I cannot describe the depth of my disgust about the whole thing. I managed to keep calm at Aunty Susan's because I didn't want an undignified scene. Jon, on the other hand, told them exactly what *he* thought of the three piece suit and bow tie they plan to put him in. He was brilliant – just the right mix of outrage and stubbornness. I gave him an encouraging smile to spur him on when no one was looking, and later I told him I was very proud of his stand. (He beamed a gappy grin and cadged twenty pence for sweets!) I've told Mum she can simply write to Eleanor and tell her the deal's off. She's too tired to do it tonight, but I'm going to make sure she does it first thing in the morning. What do they think I am?

19th May

So much for our peaceful weekend. I feel more shattered now than when I went! The children behaved abominably. We saw drawings and material samples of Jenny's dress and Jon's suit. Jenny's dress looks beautiful – full waisted, with stiff petticoats and lots of bows, plus a matching one for her hair. I know she's not fond of pink (and truthfully this is a very pink pink*) but it will look lovely on her. Jon has this adorable little suit in black velvet, complete with waistcoat and a tiny bow tie.*

Jon took one look and declared it was girls' stuff and he wouldn't wear it. It was so embarrassing. I tried to shut him up but he said plenty more, all of it on the same theme. Eleanor looked crushed. I could see Jenny open her mouth to chip in her two cents' worth, but then she changed her mind and said nothing. She settled for that awful mutinous expression that teenagers adopt when they're not pleased. Very expressive. In her case, it wasn't what she said that was embarrassing, but the way she avoided saying anything, not even a polite 'nice' in response to being shown the drawings. In fact, she looked shell-shocked. What did she think she was going to wear for heaven's sake? Jeans and a sweatshirt? This is more or less a society wedding after all; some of the stars of the shows Greg and Eleanor have worked on will be there.

Jenny started as soon as we got home. She wanted me to sit down there and then and write to Eleanor saying she couldn't be bridesmaid after all. I was so tired I couldn't bear a confrontation so I put her off. It will teach her a valuable lesson to have to go through with this wedding. It's about time she stopped seeing herself as the centre of the universe and started thinking of others. (My mother used to say that!)

Jon and I had a talk this morning. (He's grown up a lot in the last few months.) We're both going to refuse to wear Eleanor's Frankenstein costumes. She can ask someone else, or come up with a sensible idea for our clothes. We don't care which.

I told Dave and Sadie about the dress – they nearly died laughing! I thought Dave would understand, but he actually said since it was only for a day and no one from school would be there, he didn't see what all the fuss was about! Sadie was a bit more sympathetic, but she and Dave both thought I should go through with it. NO WAY! At least Cathy and her mum understood. Cathy's mum said no one has the right to make me feel a fool, and that's exactly the point. Jon and I are going to stand up for ourselves!

The wedding saga continues. Today Mum said she had no intention of letting us pull out of the wedding – we SAID we would do it and we WILL do it. The cheek of it! I'd rather die than be so humiliated. I told them exactly that. Dad said I was being over dramatic and Mum said I'd be in big trouble if I spoiled things for Eleanor. But Eleanor's spoiling things, not me. Why can't she just be sensible?

Anyway, when I got home from Dave's house (one of the rare nights they agreed to me going out on a school night, as I lost the weekend) what should I see on the dining room table but a new Lego creation built from a kit Jon's been after for ages. Of course I smelled a rat, and sure enough, the toad has agreed to wear the stupid suit in return for Lego. Thirty pieces of Lego, I expect. (That's a literary reference, as my English teacher would say.) Mum even had the cheek to offer ME a bribe – the new Madonna tape. Maybe Jon can be bought but my principles aren't so cheap. I'm not giving in.

22nd May

Jenny has been encouraging Jon in his refusal to be a page boy. They are both being very difficult, but I'm not giving in. They could have said no at the beginning, and it's just not fair on Eleanor to back out now. She was on the phone again this evening, poor thing; she keeps calling to make sure everything's all right. I expect she's worried that they'll sulk at the wedding and spoil things. They'd better not dare! I told her they were fine about it – total lie, but there's a couple of months to go yet. I'm beginning to win Jon over. I'm shamelessly bribing him with Lego. It's only a matter of time before I find the weak part of Jenny's armour; until then, I'm hoping regular threats of what will happen if she dares to spoil the wedding will do the trick.

Round at Cathy's again – it's becoming a bit of a Sunday night routine, now Dave's at work and Sadie's seeing Pete. Her mum was in this time. I think she was a bit drunk, but she wasn't violent or anything. Mum said today that I shouldn't see so much of Cathy. She thinks she's a bad influence. Just because Cathy's clothes are way-out and her mum's a bit weird, my mum's against her. Typical of parents. Cathy can't help what goes on. Her dad left them last year; she doesn't even know where he is. I know Mum's only doing what she thinks is best, but she's such a snob.

Things are easing up at work now, and Mike has been given another assistant manager, so things are looking up. We had a lovely afternoon walk – really relaxing – and then a quiet evening with Jon in bed and Jenny out at Catherine's.

I wish Jenny was a bit more discerning about her friends. Catherine seems to be a very strange girl: all black clothes, dyed black hair and deathly white face, like something from the grave. I've heard stories about her mother which make me feel very uneasy about Jenny spending so much time round there; no wonder the father left. I don't like to listen to idle gossip, but I can't help worrying about her influence on Jenny. I tried to very gently steer her in the direction of other friendships – Celia Clondyke-Smith's daughter, Helena, would be a much more suitable friend. I got nowhere. Jenny just called me a snob!

Sadie came round in floods of tears tonight – Pete dropped her. He still wants to be friends, but he doesn't want to go out with her any more. They didn't even have a row. I told her he's a wimp anyway, but she's still really upset. I think she was too keen to please him; she was a bit like an eager puppy. There was an article in 'American Teen' just last week about that – 'women who love too much'. I didn't show it to Sadie, though. She's upset enough already. I feel helpless. I wish I knew what to do.

Poor Sadie – she makes me feel guilty being so happy. And this thing's also made me wonder about me and Dave. Have I been too keen? Maybe I should ease things off between us a bit. Besides, Sadie needs me now, and I can't leave her in despair. She's got no one else, and she's my best friend. I let Jon feel pushed away because I was so wrapped up in Dave. I don't want to make the same mistake with Sadie. I'm going to make more time for her, even if it does mean seeing a bit less of Dave. It will be very painful, but if the situations were reversed I know Sadie would do the same for me (NOT that Dave and I are going to split up . . .)

Spoke to Dave about Sadie. He was really good – said we would have to try and cheer her up. We're all going to the cinema, and he's offered her a free burger if she goes in when he's working. I felt a bit jealous about that – he doesn't like *me* going to the burger bar when he's at work. But I swallowed it. I should count myself lucky to have such a considerate boyfriend. Sadie actually smiled at me, so that's a good sign. Maybe she's beginning to realize that no boy is worth being miserable over.

The parents have been having a go about school work again. They say I'm starting to go out too much. The old deal of weekends only is back. I can have friends round here, but not go out. I can't wait until I'm old enough to lead my own life. Still, with Dave working and Sadie needing me, I don't suppose I'll be wanting to go out much, anyway. So I was very gracious about it. They deserve to win a small battle now and then.

Jenny's work has been falling off again. Somehow we relaxed the rule about not going out on schoolnights and she doesn't seem to be doing much homework at all. We had to lay down the ground rules afresh. I expected the usual scene, but she was amazingly mature about it – said she could see our point, and agreed quite calmly to stay in on schoolnights as long as she could have friends round sometimes. This seemed reasonable – I was so shocked at her reaction I would probably have agreed to all sorts of things at that moment!

I wonder if this new maturity will stretch to cheerfully wearing a certain pink dress — somehow I doubt it.

So much for Sadie needing me – I've hardly seen her at all the last few days, except at school. She's not home when I telephone; she says she's going for long walks or even the cinema on her own! I though she might have a new boyfriend and wants to keep him secret, but Dave says no. He's seen her in the burger bar a couple of times, alone. I've told him to be nice to her – she must be going through a very difficult patch. Dave suddenly kissed me. He said I was a very understanding person, and it was one of the reasons he loved me! He's never actually said the words before – he's too shy. I feel on top of the moon. I love him like mad, and I never want this feeling to end.

The wedding is coming up fast. Mum has really laid the law down, and I've got to go through with it. At least no one important will see me looking such a twit. Some actors and stuff are going to be there, but none of the names Mum mentioned meant anything to me (probably BBC 2 types) so I don't mind them seeing me in my Shame.

16th June

Jenny has been playing nursemaid to her friend Sadie, whose boyfriend has decided to be 'just good friends'. I think it's shaken Jenny a bit, although she assures me that Dave would never do anything like that to her. I hope she's right. Why does learning about love have to be so painful? Why can't we all just meet the right person straight away and settle down? All this experimentation seems so messy and unnecessary. Whoever said teenage years are the most exciting needs his head examining.

I am looking forward to Eleanor's wedding. Jon is quite excited about it now, too. We've told him how important the page boy is in a wedding(!) Jenny is sullen but silent on the subject of the pink dress, which I have made clear is going to be worn by her, come what may. It crossed my mind that she might pretend to be ill on the day, so I told her that only something nasty enough to keep her in bed for a week – and away from her precious Dave, of course – will count as a real illness. She hadn't even thought of it – what's this generation coming to?

Cathy and I have been together a lot the last couple of weeks. I feel a bit as though I'm using her because Sadie's not around and Dave's busy with work, but she doesn't seem to mind. We had this really weird conversation tonight. I was telling her that I envy her because her mum is so easy going and mine's a dragon lady. Then Cathy said SHE envied ME! She LIKES my parents – says they're great! I told her I would swop (and I was only half joking!) and she said if she went missing one night, her mum wouldn't even notice until well into the next day. Even then she probably wouldn't call the police for another day after that.

The funny thing was, when she went home and I sat and thought about it, I realized Cathy's right. Her mum only lets her do what she likes because she doesn't want the bother of having her around. Cathy says half the time her mum doesn't know whether Cathy's in the house or not – she's too drunk. That must feel awful. I wouldn't really want Cathy's life. Even mine's an improvement on that. At least Mum and Dad only nag because they care what happens to me.

Mum finished the wedding cake tonight. They say love is blind – so with any luck Eleanor will be too starry-eyed to look at it closely! (Only joking – it looks surprisingly OK, considering.)

Just got back from Eleanor's – the wedding was incredible!! I hope I'm not too tired to get it all down before I fall asleep.

First, Eleanor. She looked so beautiful it made you want to cry – Aunty Susan and Mum DID cry. They sobbed together all through the ceremony. It was so embarrassing. I could forgive Aunty Susan – the bride's mum has to cry, it's all part of the tradition. But Mum's only an aunty. She hasn't even seen that much of Eleanor. I tried glaring at her as I went up the aisle. But she just gave me this watery smile and cried even more. You can't take parents anywhere; I just tried to pretend I wasn't with her.

Eleanor's dress was lovely. I have made my feelings about the bridesmaids' outfits clear already. Let's just say that when you saw FOUR of us dressed in the ghastly things, with backcombed hair and little flowers all over the place, it was even worse. We looked like something that had sprouted up from another planet.

I was in charge of the other three bridesmaids, and Jon. He, for once, was as good as gold. He looked so cute. But the bridesmaids were horrid creatures. One of them, Greg's niece, kept trying to get a drink at the bar. When that didn't work, she went round sipping other people's drinks when they weren't looking. I told her she'd get sick, but she said she could 'hold her liquor'. She's only eight! (I'm beginning to understand what too much telly can do to a person.)

There was no wedding car – Eleanor lives near the church, so the idea was to walk, with the bridesmaids in front throwing down rose petals. Very romantic. Unfortunately it rained. Eleanor's dad produced these awful bootee things – galoshes, he called them. They looked like disposable wellies – very fetching with the salmon pink. What with those and the golf umbrellas, we looked a real sight marching down the street. If anyone from school had seen me, I would have died on the spot. I tossed the rose petals too fast – they were all gone before we were halfway to the church. I felt really sorry for Eleanor, but she didn't seem to mind. She just laughed. I hope I can be so good-hearted when it's my turn . . .

I couldn't wait to get back into my jeans and T-shirt at the end of the day – but I felt good about having made such a noble sacrifice for the sake of Eleanor's happiness. Can't write any more – too tired. Will get to the reception tomorrow.

6th July

Eleanor's wedding was marvellous, despite some quite heavy rain. There was a sort of procession of family and friends from Eleanor and Greg's house to the church nearby. Jenny walked ahead of the wedding couple, scattering rose petals. Apparently it's a continental custom. It was very romantic, although the fact that they had to wear galoshes and have umbrellas meant it was not as picturesque as one might have wished. Still, Eleanor and Greg were oblivious to the rain; their faces shone with joy.

As they walked down the aisle Susan started to cry, which brought tears to my eyes, too. It is a long time since I last saw Jenny in a dress. She looked so grown-up and beautiful it quite took my breath away. Mike slipped his hand into mine and I knew he was proud of her, just as I was. You bring your children into the world as dependent little bundles, and you nurture them into grown-up people whom you know will inevitably leave you. It's wonderful and sad at the same time.

One day Jenny will hopefully walk down the aisle of our church on the arm of the man she loves, and our lives will never again be shared in the way they are now.

As I was thinking this, Jenny passed by our pew. She turned to me and the look on her face told me she was thinking exactly the same thing. She could feel how near she was to adulthood and the leavetaking, and excitement and anguish mixed on her face. It was one of those rare moments of mother and daughter communication, and it finished me off. I needed a whole packet of Kleenex to get through the service after that.

The reception was lovely. The children behaved impeccably. Jon was very cute, and didn't whine once. In fact, I hardly saw him during the reception. I truly think Jenny was surprised at how pretty she looked in the dress, after all that fuss, and enjoyed being looked at and complimented. Maybe it will encourage her to dress a little more becomingly in the future. Mike and I had a chance to relive our courting days – we started off with Fifties stuff, at Eleanor's request, but before long we were mashing potatoes, twisting, mod-marching etc. – all the dances we were crazy for in our youth. It was brilliant. I bet Jenny was surprised to see how well Mike can dance! He could still give any teenager a run for their money.

Still tired from yesterday, but had a reasonably restful day today. I went round Dave's to watch a video ('Ghost' – for the third time, but I didn't tell Dave that). Sadie was there, too. She seemed surprised to see me – she thought we were all staying the whole weekend at Aunty Susan's. She'd only dropped by to bring a record back, but she wasn't doing anything so we all watched the film together.

Dave seemed a bit strange. He was pleased to see me, and kissed me hello. But he didn't kiss me any more until I left, and then it wasn't the usual sort of kiss. He must have been a bit embarrassed because of Sadie. I expect it's hard for her to see us kissing when she's got no one. Dave's very sensitive about other people's feelings (that's ONE of the things I love about him).

Back to the reception. The actual service was fine (once the galoshes and brollies were stowed away) and the reception at the hotel was FANTASTIC. Loads of posh food and lovely fruit punch, wine and champagne flowing like water. Dad made a bit of a fool of himself dancing some weird routine from his youth. The oldies all lined up and did strange dances together (inspired by the Fifties theme) including one called 'March of the Mods' which was apparently not even a Fifties dance. As far as I could see, it involved just stomping up and down the room. Needless to say MY parents were there in the thick of it. I pretended I had come on my own. Jon met up with another little boy but they were no trouble. They spent the whole time cruising the food tables. It's a wonder Jon wasn't sick.

Only ten more days of term and then six whole weeks of holiday. The teachers have given up moaning and started looking cheerful. We're not getting so much homework, although English and History projects have to be done in the holiday.

My end-of-year report was not at all bad. There was the usual rash of 'could do better's' (even in History, which is unfair because Dave and I SLAVED over the coursework last term) but on the whole they reckoned I could get at least a 'B' next year, except Latin (border-line C). Miss Willis (English) even predicted a possible 'A' – says I have a 'Lively imagination and fluid style', no less. Dad says I get that from his side of the family. His uncle wrote letters to the 'Times' every single week for years, and Dad had a poem published in the school magazine back in the dark ages!

Enough of all that. The sun is shining, freedom beckons and Dave and I will have all those long days TOGETHER.

Dave and I had our first proper row tonight. We made it up before he walked me home, but it was awful.

We were at the youth club, with Sadie. She and Dave were playing table tennis together. They've entered the club tournament, mixed doubles. Dave asked me first, but Sadie's much better and had no partner. So I did the noble thing and dropped out. Now I wish I hadn't – they take the whole thing too seriously, and they practise all the time. I know Dave's trying to be kind to Sadie, but he doesn't need to go over the top, does he?

What I wanted was to go for a walk, just me and Dave, and plan the holidays. He wouldn't come – said he wanted to play table tennis. I got a bit miffed, and went outside to play volleyball. When I came back in, Dave was just sitting at the edge with Sadie and a couple of other people, talking. It seemed like he would talk to them but didn't want to talk to me.

When I finally did get him on his own and told him my ideas for the school holidays, he said it wasn't good to plan so much time together. He's already arranged to do things with other people. He's going youth hostelling for three days with a couple of boys from school, and I didn't even know! By the time I've been away for two weeks that means most of the holiday will be gone. I suppose I got really mad then. Somehow it blew up into a row and he said I was being childish and possessive. That really hurt! I started crying. He put his arm round me and said sorry and we kissed and stuff. But I still don't know how the row happened, or who started it. Maybe I am too possessive, but I love him so much I don't want to be with anyone else. I wish he felt the same way about me.

Jon's school report came back today. He has obviously made a big impression on his teacher this year. She thinks he's a little angel. Wish she could see him at home! Jenny's end-of-year report last week was also a pleasant surprise. It wasn't as bad as we had feared. The coursework seems to be moving at a reasonable pace. The real test will come in December when she faces the mock exams. They don't have any exams in the fourth year, to give maximum time for coursework. Personally I think the discipline of preparing for exams would have stood Jenny in good stead this year, and given her something else to think about apart from David Slater.

There seems to be something up. Things have been very tense with Jenny today. It's like walking on eggshells — the least little thing sends her into a rage. Jon went into her room, just to see if she had any washing-up in there, and you would have thought he'd committed a major crime, poor thing. She came home very subdued last night, and I wonder if things are going wrong with David. She says they didn't have a fight or anything, but things are not right. I hope she's not heading for a fall with that young man. It's bound to end sooner or later, I suppose — it's highly unlikely that kids of that age will stay together for life, but selfishly I hope it's Jenny who gets tired first. No sign of that at the moment!

Things have been OK with Dave since the row. We talked about the holidays a bit more sensibly. Now I've thought about it I know he's right, we shouldn't just depend on each other. We'll still have lots of time together, and I don't want to lose my friends. Sadie and I do have a lot of fun. We've been through so much. I know we'll be friends all our lives, wherever we are.

I'm going to be busy looking after Jon, too, when Mum is at work. She's been rushing about a lot lately and she looks tired. This will be the first year I'm really in charge – the last couple of years Jean next door has 'happened' to pop in now and then. It'll be good practice for me when I have a family . . .!

So, things are all set for the summer holidays. If only they would hurry up and COME!!!

18th July

Last peaceful day before the school holidays begin and chaos reigns. I was on the morning shift today, and when I got home from work I sat in the garden and did absolutely nothing. I need to build up my store of patience for the next six weeks. Having the children home is absolutely wonderful, for a couple of weeks. From then on, it's steadily downhill. Jenny has agreed to looking after Jon while I'm at work more readily than usual, which was a surprise.

Things have eased a bit with Jenny. I think something must have happened between her and Dave, or one of her friends, to make her so tense; whatever it was must have been resolved somehow. I must admit I was very worried for a while. I even wondered if she might be pregnant, horrid suspicious old mother that I am.

In the book Mum bought me for Christmas (How to Handle Your Teenager) it urged full and frank discussion of girl/boyfriends, including making sure your child knows about birth control and so on. Well, I tried. I know everyone is supposed to be able to say 'condom' quite openly now – its almost a requirement to mention them thrice daily in some circles. Even Jon knows what they are, although he has only a hazy idea of what they're used for. It's all good stuff, this openness and frank talking about sex. I just can't bring myself to DO it (the talking, I mean). I'm sure Jenny wouldn't do anything daft, and things haven't got that far – but am I just saying that to save myself the worry? I'm very confused.

I wish I had talked to Jenny properly about AIDS and birth control and being careful and all that kind of thing – not just those quick explanations I gave her when she was eleven and not really interested. The trouble is, if I do it now it will look as if I'm suspicious about what's going between Jenny and Dave. Well, I AM suspicious, of course, but I'd rather keep the veneer of the trusting mother for the moment. So I'm keeping my fingers crossed and trying not to think about it!

David dumped me today. I can hardly believe it. He's started going out with Sadie. She's supposed to be my best friend, but best friends don't behave like that, do they?

I go cold when I think of all the times I confided in Sadie – all the things I told her about me and Dave. She sat there, taking it all in, and all the time she was scheming to get him for herself! And I HELPED her – I actually ASKED Dave to be nice to her. She must have been laughing at me all the time.

That's not what *she* says, of course. *She* says they couldn't help it – they just 'fell in love'. It makes me sick to think of them together. Well, she'll learn. He said he loved me – now he's gone off with her. He'll dump her too, soon as he finds out she's not as smart and sexy as he thinks she is.

Dave didn't even have the guts to tell me himself. He wrote a note, and dropped it through the door. No mention of Sadie: just saying he was sorry. He'll always 'like me as a friend', but that's all. So I go charging off to Sadie, to cry on her shoulder. That's what your best friend's for, isn't it?

It was so humiliating. She thought I already knew – kept saying I must have suspected. Well I didn't. How could I? She's my best friend, and Dave's the boy I love. How could I know they'd pull such a dirty trick? Sadie was crying, and said she was sorry. I don't care. I just left. I never want to see either of them again.

Now I face the rest of the school holiday completely alone. We had planned all sorts of things together – Dave and me, Sadie and me. Now I've got nothing. He could at least have waited until the holidays were over. I'll never trust anyone again. They can all go to hell. I'll make new friends, but I won't ever let anyone get as

Oh God! I know I told her about the STORK when she was FOUR... but did I ever tell her about the REAL stuff?
Should I go all the way with him?
MORE SEX NEXT WEEK!
Mstake
SPECIAL SEX issue
Do they use CONDOMS?
Would he DROP me if I didn't? Would he DROP me if I did? Would I like it, anyway?
Could she be PREGNANT?!
Maybe I should wait until he kisses me, THEN decide....

close as they did. I'm not going to hurt like this again for anybody.

When I got home from Sadie's, Mum was waiting. I cried and cried, and she hugged me and didn't even ask what had happened. It was as if she knew about Sadie; she was really great. She didn't say there were plenty more fish in the sea, like I expected her to. She made a pot of tea, flourished a pack of chocolate marshmallows under my nose (my favourites, when I'm not in Despair) and listened to everything I said without interrupting.

Then she told me about the first boy who ever dumped *her*. It was centuries ago and he sounded a right wally anyway. But she loved him at the time. When she was telling me how she'd felt, what they'd said to each other, it was just the sort of things I said and felt. It's amazing. Mum might be old, but she knows more than I thought she did. I'm not sure how I can go on without Dave, but I'm blowed if I'm going to show how I feel in front of them. I'll do my crying in private. And I hope Sadie doesn't think she can come running to me when she finds out what sort of a creep David Slater really is!

1st August

Jenny and David broke up today. Poor Jenny; he wasn't very chivalrous about it. He wrote a note and pushed it through the door. I don't suppose he has any more experience of all this than she does. I had an idea things weren't going too well; nothing I could put my finger on, but there has been something awkward between them lately. Once or twice when Sadie was here with Jenny and David, Sadie seemed suspiciously coy. I suppose I knew she liked David, but I pushed it out of my mind, not wanting it to be true. In any case, Jenny didn't seem to be at all worried; they even went out in a three some-times.

85

When the note came, Jenny read it and handed it to me without a word. I followed her upstairs, but she didn't want to talk; she was putting on her trainers and combing her hair. When she told me she was going to see Sadie, I could tell she had no suspicion – unlike her cynical mother – that Sadie might already know. I wanted to warn her, but how could I? After all, I might be wrong. So I let her go.

I told Mike he should perhaps take Jon out to the park for a game of football or something. He just raised his eyebrows and said fine. He's such a love. I'm sure he finds half of what goes on between Jenny and me quite mystifying; his relationship with her is so blissfully uncomplicated!

I nipped out to the corner shop and bought some of Jenny's favourite biscuits for a spot of comfort eating, then settled down to wait. I remembered Rory McLaughlin, the most handsome boy in the school and my first love. When he threw me over for another girl I thought the world had crumbled. People kept telling me to cheer up, find someone else, but as far as I was concerned that was like telling a man with no legs to jump up and dance.

He wasn't the last boy to let me down, either. I never learned. I spent those years before meeting Mike in a swingboat of exhilaration and despair. I wouldn't want to be a teenager again for all the tea in China.

When Jenny came back, all stony face and stiff shoulders, I wanted to cry. She looked like a crumpled little girl. But soon she'll be a woman, and all this is part of the process.

For once, Jenny and I really talked – proper woman-to-woman stuff. I even told her about Rory. I feel awful for Jenny, but I will treasure this afternoon because it has shown me how lovely it will be to have a grown-up daughter, sharing on equal terms. And it showed me that Jenny is strong – she'll survive. I am proud of the way she's handling this setback; there's a bit of melodrama, but not half as much as I indulged in at her age!

The sun is shining today, but everything looks black and cold to me. I keep seeing Sadie and Dave together, in my head. They're always kissing. I want to kill them both. Last night I dreamed about murdering them. When I woke up I was scared that I might actually have done it. Perhaps I've gone mad. All those stories I've read about jilted brides who became insane – perhaps they're true. My boyfriend and my best friend, together. The more I try not to picture them, the more I do. Why would two of the most important people in my life do that to me? I must be stupid, worthless and ugly. I can't write any more.

I wonder how my mother felt when Rory and I split up. She never said, and I never asked. Now that I have Jenny I can see that must have been hurtful sometimes. It's not easy to stand back from a teenager's life and watch them stumbling about, making all the mistakes you made. You want to catch them as they fall, and wrap them in a protective shield so no one can hurt them. But then, how would they learn? So you force yourself to stand back, hoping they'll ask for help when they can't cope alone. That's the hardest part.

The closeness of a couple of days ago seems to have gone. Jenny is withdrawn, silent, in a world of her own. I can't reach her. A couple of times I found her looking at me, or standing by me, and I felt she needed to say something. But nothing has come of it. I don't know what to do. If I ask her to tell me what she's feeling, she'll think I'm prying. But it's almost worse waiting for her to speak first.

We are off to Scotland in a couple of days. Lots of long walks and the beautiful scenery will have a healing effect – I hope so, anyway.

I wanted to talk to Mum, to try and tell her about the dreams – they haven't stopped. But first she was busy with Jon, and then she kept telling me to cheer up. She says I'll feel better when we go on holiday. It's like that afternoon when we talked didn't really happen. She seems to think I'll just pull out of it, that one talk and a cuddle was enough. How can she be so understanding one minute and so thick the next? Now I feel like I've got no one in the whole world.

Sadie phoned today. I put the phone down on her.

I will have to stop looking in the mirror. I feel bad

enough inside, without being reminded how awful I look as well. My skin is all lumpy and pale, just right for showing up the red of a crop of spots on my chin. My eyes are all puffy and my hair looks like tangled knitting. To top it all, my period started this morning. Plenty more fish in the sea, they say. I feel like a bloated whale. No one will ever look at me again without flinching. What a holiday this is turning out to be.

We've been here in Scotland for nearly a week. It has been grey and rainy all the time. The sky knows how I feel; it's crying for me. The days seem to go on for ever. All I want to do is sleep, but Mum keeps dragging me out. So what? Nothing matters any more.

14th August

The holiday is half-way through. There's been no time to write anything down. The days have been packed. We've been walking, sailing, fishing, shopping, seen some magnificent castles, even hunted the Loch Ness monster. The weather has not been bad on the whole. There has been some light rain, but nothing that's stopped us.

Everything would be lovely if only Jenny would cheer up. Her misery has become self-indulgent, as though she's watching herself on screen playing a part. She rarely speaks, doesn't want to do anything, comes along with us only because she has to etc. It has set everyone on edge. Even Jon is affected. He keeps trying to cheer her up with pictures, and flowers he has picked. He even offers to share his sweets with her. She just shakes her head or ignores him. Part of me wants to shake her and part wants to cry for her.

Mum and Dad and Jon are having a whale of a time. No one seems to notice me any more. I just wish I could die, quickly and painlessly. I couldn't actually kill myself, but I wouldn't mind being suddenly dead. Life doesn't seem worth much. I bet Sadie and Dave are having a good time. Here I go again. I can't think of anything else.

17th August

Jenny continues to do her best to spoil the holiday. Mike snapped this evening. He had tried to get her to say where she wanted to go tomorrow, but all she would say was that it 'didn't matter'. Mike got more and more annoyed (I don't think she even noticed) and then shouted at her. He said she was spoiling the holiday for everyone and it was time she snapped out of it. She didn't even respond. I thought he was being too hard on her, and said so. Mike started shouting at me, then, saying I was letting her get away with playing the dramatic heroine and he was fed up with it. So we shouted at each other, Jon started crying, Jenny went upstairs and wouldn't come down – it was awful. Some holiday. We may as well have stayed at home.

We go home tomorrow. I've tried my best to snap out of my misery, but it's hard. Yesterday, though, I made a start. We had a boat trip out to a little island, and saw some seals. When we headed back towards the harbour, the sun was setting. It was beautiful. It got me thinking about how the sea and the sky and the mountains go on for ever, and how tiny and unimportant human beings are. Whatever happens to us, however long our lives, they are just like the blink of an eye in the world's timescale. It was an amazing thought. When we got back to the hotel I wrote a poem about it. Writing it all down makes me feel a bit better; it's comforting. I'm going to write down everything I feel, and then burn the paper. Perhaps the bad feelings will burn away with it.

The holiday is over, thank God. I can't say it was restful, or an experience I would wish to repeat. Next year we'll send the children to Mum's and go on our own. What with Jenny indulging in grand dollops of despair and Jon whining even more than usual (probably because of all the tension, if I'm fair) it was not worth the bother.

Although it was a disaster for the rest of us, the holiday does at least seem to have done Jenny some good. Towards the end of our stay she began to be a bit brighter. You could sometimes get as many as five words at a time. But now we're home she spends a lot of time up in her room, no doubt staring into space and thinking of her long-lost love. The sooner she gets back to school and back to some hard graft, the better.

Back to school tomorrow. I'm dreading it. Sadie and Dave will be flaunting themselves. Everyone will know what's happened. It's so humiliating. Being dropped by someone you love and trust is bad enough, without everyone gawping and whispering behind their hands. I told Mum I couldn't face it, but she said I'd have to sometime – not turning up tomorrow will give the gossips a head start. I suppose she's right. I'm going to have to be brave. I still have SOME friends left, and they'll see me through. I'm not looking forward to it, though.

Mum and Dad have been pretty good really. Even Jon feels for me – he brings me little pictures he's done. I am lucky to have my family around me, not like Cathy. We've been going around quite a lot together since I got back from Scotland. Mum doesn't like it, but that's just snobbery and she knows it, so she doesn't actually say anything just looks disapproving when I mention Cathy's name.

There was a note from Sadie the day I got back, and one yesterday too, asking me to phone or go round. I tore them up. I can't forgive her. I think she's got a nerve expecting me to.

Jenny was very subdued all evening. I asked how school went, but could get nothing more than a shrug and an 'OK'. It must have been a nightmare. We all tried to show our support: I cooked Lasagne, which is usually her favourite (she didn't eat much), Mike didn't complain about sacrificing the News to yet another TV soap, and Jon drew her a little card with 'Best Bigg Sisstar' on the front, and loads of kisses on the inside. She didn't claim the kisses, but she managed a clumsy hug. I think, at last, she is on her way back from the depths.

Weird evening at home — everyone tiptoeing around and being nice to each other (especially me!)

School wasn't as bad as I thought — wish I hadn't stayed awake all night worrying about it now! Dave and Sadie looked embarrassed and uncomfortable (GOOD!) A couple of the girls in my class won't even speak to Sadie, and they were all really nice to me and sort of cool to her. Helena Clondyke-Smith is the only one she can count on, and that's no loss to me. I've got really good friends, even without Sadie and Dave. That's comforting, but it doesn't fill the hole their treachery has left.

A couple of the teachers sussed it out straight away, and I could tell they felt sorry for me. So I pretended I didn't care (I'm getting quite good at that) and that it was a relief he ended it before I had to.

But in the end, it's only pretending. I still cry inside, all the time.

I went to a new youth club tonight, with Cathy. It was OK. At least Sadie and Dave weren't there. One of the boys from the sixth form was there, and we got talking. He seems quite nice. His name's Chris, and he's into scuba diving, of all things.

Talking of boys, Pete Kelly (the one who dropped Sadie) asked me out! I said yes – we're going bowling on Saturday. I'm not really interested in Pete, but he's OK. And I can't wait for a word to get back to Sadie (which of course it will). It'll really show David Slater how easy it is to recover from him, too.

Sadie phoned again tonight. I talked to her this time – I told her to leave me alone. THEN I put the phone down on her!

I do miss her, though. I even feel a bit sorry for her – she's caught between Dave and me, and maybe she didn't mean for all this to happen. It's going to be hard to ignore her for ever.

Just got back from bowling with Pete. He's OK but he's not Dave. Next week we're going to the fair together, but I think I made it clear I'm not after anything serious. I didn't want to hurt him, or use him to get at Dave, so I had to say something. I told him I thought it was a bad idea to get too involved with someone from the same year – leads to complications. He said he knew exactly what I meant!

Cathy wants me to go to a new night club that's opening in town. You have to be 18, but she says we'll get in. I've heard these places can be a bit rough, and I'm not that keen. But I don't want to be a wally, either.

Jenny has taken up with Catherine Davies again. She appears to be more cheerful, but I wish she could find someone else to go about with. I think Sadie is trying to make up, but Jenny won't have it. She's very unforgiving. One day the boot will be on the other foot and she'll realize life is just not as simple as she wants it to be.

She's going out with another boy, the one who threw Sadie over. It's a spiteful action – she doesn't have any interest in the poor lad, and is just using him to get back at Sadie. I don't like admitting my daughter could be so callous, but I'm pretty sure that's what it's about. I wouldn't be surprised if Catherine gave her the idea.

Went to the youth club with Cathy. She wants me to go to the nightclub with her this Saturday. At first I said no. I knew Mum and Dad would hate it and I didn't want to go behind their backs. Cathy was OK about it, but disappointed. We stayed in the park talking for ages, and I was late home. The fuss was incredible, like I'd been selling myself on the streets or something. Mum got really snotty about Cathy, saying she was a bad influence. That did it. I'm going to the nightclub now. I'll tell Cathy tomorrow. How dare She pick my friends for me? Mum doesn't understand Cathy at all, she's never given her a chance. She's just a snob.

24th September

Yet another showdown with Jenny. She went off with Catherine to some youth club, and was more than an hour late home. This, in some mysterious way, was apparently MY fault. Mike and I are too restrictive, and invite trouble by not allowing her any freedom. It sounded like something Catherine would come up with, and I said so. I asked if she wanted the sort of freedom Catherine had, while her mother was putting herself about all over town.

I went cold even writing that bit down. It was a terrible thing to say, but I couldn't call the words back. I am ashamed of myself. Jenny stormed out with a face like thunder, after calling me a twisted and bitter old snob.

This must be the worst day of my whole life. I hate Mum, and she hates me too. I wish I could just run away and never come back.

Cathy and I went to 'Upstarts' – we got in easily. I told Mum and Dad I was going to the cinema with Annie. (Mum likes Annie – she's very 'respectable'.) I told her Annie's dad was collecting us afterwards. She swallowed it whole.

At first, it was really good. The music was great, and the people were much more sophisticated than the usual schoolkid gaggle. Then these two blokes asked us to dance. They were quite a bit older than us. Cathy told them we were nearly eighteen, but I felt nervous and wished they would go away. Anyway, we went to the bar together and they bought us drinks. I asked for Coke, but Cathy said, 'Rum and Coke, she means' and flashed me this awful look. It tasted foul, but I felt like a wally so I had to try and drink it. Cathy was getting stuck into her fourth vodka when her bloke, Steve, started groping her. She didn't even seem to mind. I was landed with Tony, who works in an electronics factory. He didn't grope, but there was nothing else about him I liked. (I told him I worked in a greengrocers' shop. I used to, on Saturdays!)

When we went to the loo, I told Cathy she should back off – they were a lot older, and she was getting drunk. I was worried about what she would do. I asked her to come home, but she wouldn't, and I couldn't leave her there on her own. So we stayed. Tony asked me to dance, and I said no. I said he could ask someone else if he wanted – and he did! I felt really stupid, sitting watching the others. Cathy got into heavy kissing. She was out of her skull. I wanted to phone Dad to come, but I knew he would be furious about me even being there. So I couldn't.

Around eleven, I got really worried. I dragged Cathy off to the loo again and told her I had to get home soon or there'd be trouble. She wouldn't come. So we had a row. Then she put her arm round me and said I should lighten up for once, and have some fun. In other words, I'm a drag to be with most of the time!

In the end I left. There was a man at the bus stop, so I walked. I was scared stiff. The roads were dark and I had to walk down an alley and across the park. I was terrified someone would grab me. I suppose I could have phoned, even then. But the fuss Mum and Dad would make would be even worse than the fear of being grabbed.

By the time I got home I was exhausted. My mascara was all runny from crying. I was worried to death about Cathy and those men, and I didn't know what to do. I really wanted to tell Mum and Dad, and get some help. But as soon as I saw them I knew there was no chance. They were furious. I didn't even get a chance to explain. Mum had gone through my things and got my address book – she'd spoken to Annie's dad.

You'd think they'd be glad I was safe, but not them. They just kept on and on and on at me. I told them I'd changed my mind about the cinema and gone out with friends. I wouldn't tell them anything else (except that it was none of their business, which didn't go down well).

They've stopped my pocket money and grounded me for a month. I think Dad would have listened if I'd told them the truth, but I've never seen Mum so angry. She looked at me as though she wished I'd never been born. So do I.

I hope Cathy's all right. She was too drunk to know what she was doing. I'll never forgive myself if something happened to her because I left her there on her own.

It's 5 a.m. and I can't sleep. We had a terrible row with Jenny, and I think we handled it all wrong (me, mostly). She said she was going to the cinema with Annie, whose dad would bring them back. I was quite relieved – at least she was with someone trustworthy. She said she'd be back by eleven. I though she was being very responsible, in line with the long discussion we had last week about such things.

We have talked to Jenny many times about the importance of knowing where she is in case there's an emergency and we need to contact her. She must know, too, though I can't bring myself to say it, that part of the reason is that if something happens to her and she doesn't come home, we know when and where to start looking. On the whole, she's pretty good about it. So of course, when eleven, then half-past, came and went we began to worry. By midnight we couldn't stand the anxiety, so I went to Jenny's room and got her address book to phone Annie's house and see if they were there.

Annie's father sounded completely bewildered; I think he was in bed. I told him what Jenny had told me. There was an awful silence, and then he told me Annie was in bed – she hadn't been out all evening. He sounded very sympathetic, but I expect he wondered what sort of parents we were to let our daughter roam around until the early hours.

Mike looked shellshocked when I told him. He wanted to get the car out and scour the streets. But where would he start? We decided to wait another half hour, and then call the police. We sat in the kitchen, waiting. It was the most awful half hour of my life. I kept picturing Jenny as she had been when she left: smiling, full of life with her cheek-brusher of a kiss and a cheery wave. Then I started picturing her in a dark wood with a knife at her throat, or lying in a ditch. The more I tried to blot them out, the more pictures there were.

She turned up with five minutes to go before we called the police. Something had happened: she'd been crying and she looked as though a tram had run over her. But she was back, she was in one piece, and I wanted to hug her and kiss her and hug her some more.

So why didn't I? I don't know. Suddenly all the joy and relief was swept away by a cold rage that seemed to come from nowhere. I wanted to throttle her. She didn't seem to care that we had been out of our minds. I can't remember what I said next. I know it was too much. Mike was a bit calmer – he grounded her for a month and stopped half her pocket money this week. Then she stomped off to bed in a huff. So we still don't know where she was, or what happened to her. I doubt she'll tell us now. I've made it almost impossible for her to confide anything. I feel as though we are all trapped in a great, sticky maze, unable to reach each other. How can simply loving a child end up so disastrously?

The parents are still going around with dead-stone faces. Trying to get a conversation going is like trying to open a can with your fingernails. I realize how scared they must have been, with all the stories you hear about girls of my age being kidnapped or raped. I feel bad about putting them through that. But I've said I'm sorry – I don't know what else to do. Being grounded is bad enough, but knowing they don't trust me hurts even more. I wish I could explain what happened, but there's no point. I did the best I could do at the time, but they won't see it – they're always ready to believe the worst. (When I have kids, I'm not going to be like that.)

Cathy got home safely – her new boyfriend brought her home in his car. I told her she was stupid accepting a lift from someone she didn't know. He could have been a rapist. Cathy just laughed!

She wants me to go again, next week, but I said no. I don't care if she does think I'm a kid, I'm not going to go through another experience like that one again.

6th October

Things have been a bit tense today. I keep wanting to make contact with Jenny, but find I can't. Whether it's because of her defiant expression or my own bottled up anger that she could have been so inconsiderate, I don't know. If she would only start to talk to me, tell me what really went on last night, everything would be OK. But at the moment there's this awful wall of silence.

Jon has been very sweet today. He always is, when Jenny's in trouble, as if to show her up even more, but today's been different. He's been sweet to her as well. He knows that Jenny is not happy, and he's trying to help. But I don't think she wants any of us at the moment.

David has dumped Sadie – just the same way he did me. Apparently, he is *now* going out with a third year girl. Sadie was going round school today with puffy eyes and a sad dog expression. I wanted to speak to her, but I couldn't. The words just stuck in my throat. Betrayal is not paid for that easily. But I can't gloat over her misery, either. Last month I couldn't wait for them to split, it would have made my day. But now it's happened I just remember how awful I felt, before I came to my senses and realized that David Slater is a creep who isn't worth shedding tears over. I hope Sadie gets to see that too.

Cathy's mum's been ill, and now she has to go into hospital – there's something wrong with her liver. Cathy says it's the drink. She started to cry when she told me – she said Social Services won't let her stay in the house on her own, and she can't track down her dad.

I said she could stay with us. The words slipped out before I could think, and Cathy jumped at the chance. She's going to bring her stuff round tomorrow night, and the Social Worker will telephone Mum to make sure it's all right. That'll come as a bit of a surprise, if I don't tell her first. She's going to hit the roof!

Jenny came home from school today in a very strange mood. I couldn't work out whether she was happy or sad, wanted to talk or be left alone. While I was cooking dinner she hung around in the kitchen and seemed to be on the verge of opening a conversation. But whenever I asked her if she wanted anything, she said no. I just don't know what to make of her these days. Is this going to be the way it is for the next few years? Heaven help us.

I'll never understand parents. They're such contrary creatures. I wonder if being a parent turns your brain, or if it's actually only the weird people who becomes parents in the first place – one of life's great mysteries.

I put off telling Mum until the last possible moment. I just didn't know how to ask her. If it had been Sadie, no problem. But Cathy . . . Anyway, I had to ask in the end. When I told her what was going on with Cathy's mum, she said OK – straight away. She told me to clean the spare room and make sure Cathy brought her door key, in case she needed to get back into her house while her mum was away. She even said that she or Dad would take her up to the hospital to visit!

That's not all. Mum and Cathy are good friends! They sat up talking last night after I'd gone to bed. Cathy told me this morning that she thought Mum and Dad were great – they've helped her a lot. Wonders never cease.

I've been reading back over the last few months, and I can see that I've been rotten about them from time to time. They do their best – they get it wrong sometimes but they always think about what's best for me. I'd rather have that than Cathy's parents who are so wrapped up in themselves they just leave her to grow up completely on her own.

13th October

Cathy has been staying with us for a few days. Her mother has gone into hospital. They say her liver is giving out – she's an alcoholic, and I gather she hasn't taken care of herself at all. Nor of Cathy, poor child.

When Jenny asked me if Cathy could stay with us, it was almost as if she was throwing out a challenge. I don't think she expected me to say yes. It's a bit hurtful to think that Jenny doesn't credit me with enough compassion to take in a child in an emergency, even one I may not wholly approve of. But anyway, of course I said she could stay as long as she needed to. At the time, I was just being charitable, but now that I know Cathy better I can see that fate has thrown a real learning experience into my lap.

For a start, I misjudged Cathy. I thought she was wild and uncaring; in fact, she is desperate for attention and affection. She has been neglected in all sorts of ways. Her own mother loves her, you can see that by the way her face lights up when we take Cathy to visit. But I think it's been a long time since Cathy was properly cared for. She has blossomed here. She smiles, she talks to me much more than Jenny does, she's great with Jon and she even laughs at Mike's jokes. We have had long talks, sometimes into the night, and I realize now that she isn't wild, she just lacks direction and guidance. She has asked for advice on what to do when her mother comes out of hospital, and all sorts of things. I wish Jenny would share some of her secrets with me. It feels so good to be trusted to come up with the answers. I promised Cathy that we would help all we could, and that she would always be welcome here. Having Cathy here has helped Jenny too, in some strange way. She is much more relaxed, and is actually being quite nice to us all. Perhaps the 'terrible teens' are drawing to a close. Hallelujah!

Today I spoke to Sadie at break. It wasn't very dramatic. I stood behind her in the dinner queue and pointed out that the chips looked soggy, as usual, and she agreed. But we smiled at each other. It's a start.

I feel very mature, having written all that stuff down the other day. I haven't been much of a daughter/sister/friend sometimes. But I've really grown up in the last few months. What's happened with David, and with Cathy, has helped me sort out a few things in my list of priorities. I hope I've emerged from all this misery a nicer person.

One thing I know now is that boys shouldn't come before proper friends. That's why I talked to Sadie. Maybe we will never be as close again, but it's stupid to throw away all those years we've been best friends. And although they're a real pain at times, I know I'm lucky to have my family.

As for David Slater – I'm saving all my leftover immaturity for his especial benefit. I bet that together Sadie and I can think of a hundred and one ways to make him suffer!

GREAT! YOU'VE JUST RUINED THE REST OF MY LIFE

'My mother and father are planning to ship us all over to Canada for FOUR WHOLE MONTHS! Never mind my whole life being mucked up . . .' – Jenny, January 12th

'As anticipated, Jenny's reaction was all shock, horror, woe is me!' – Jenny's mother, January 12th

But once in Canada Jenny discovers that the move might not be such a bad thing after all, especially when she meets her next door neighbour, Dirk . . .

In this brilliant sequel to the best-selling *Not Dressed Like That, You Don't!* and *Everybody Else Does! Why Can't I?* Jenny and her mother continue to write their hilariously contrasting diaries.

BROTHER OF MINE
Chris Westwood

'Do you have any brothers or sisters?' she asked. 'A brother,' I tell her. 'But you wouldn't like him, he's nothing like me at all.'

Nick is convinced that his twin brother Tony is after everything that is his. After all, isn't Tony the one who always gets the girls, the grades and the pats on the back?

But then there is Alex, the girl at the party, and it seems at last that someone wants Nick for himself. However, when Alex mistakes Tony for Nick, Tony plays along . . .

This is a fresh, powerfully original novel from the author of *Calling all Monsters* and *A Light in the Black*.

THE GUILTY PARTY
Joan Lingard

Jodie is a fighter – and there's nothing she won't say or do to make sure that there won't be a nuclear disaster like Chernobyl in her town. It all begins harmlessly with fly-posting and peaceful protest. But then Jodie is arrested during a demonstration. Will she have the courage to go to prison for her convictions? A provocative novel about a teenager drawn into conflict with politics and the law.

DON'T LOOK BEHIND YOU

Lois Duncan

April Corrigan's life really turns into a nightmare when she learns that her father is an undercover agent for the FBI and that his cover is blown. To escape revenge from a drugs gang her father exposes, she and her family are moved from hotel to hotel, until they are finally relocated and given new identities. April's life is over. Her name, her boyfriend Steve, the tennis championships, even her long blonde hair – gone. Then one innocent attempt to regain part of her lost life sparks off a deadly series of events that threatens to destroy her new life too.

READ MORE IN PUFFIN

For children of all ages, Puffin represents quality and variety – the very best in publishing today around the world.

For complete information about books available from Puffin – and Penguin – and how to order them, contact us at the appropriate address below. Please note that for copyright reasons the selection of books varies from country to country.

On the worldwide web: www.puffin.co.uk

In the United Kingdom: Please write to *Dept. EP, Penguin Books Ltd, Bath Road, Harmondsworth, West Drayton, Middlesex UB7 ODA*

In the United States: Please write to *Consumer Sales, Penguin USA, P.O. Box 999, Dept. 17109, Bergenfield, New Jersey 07621-0120.* VISA and MasterCard holders call 1-800-253-6476 to order Penguin titles

In Canada: Please write to *Penguin Books Canada Ltd, 10 Alcorn Avenue, Suite 300, Toronto, Ontario M4V 3B2*

In Australia: Please write to *Penguin Books Australia Ltd, P.O. Box 257, Ringwood, Victoria 3134*

In New Zealand: Please write to *Penguin Books (NZ) Ltd, Private Bag 102902, North Shore Mail Centre, Auckland 10*

In India: Please write to *Penguin Books India Pvt Ltd, 706 Eros Apartments, 56 Nehru Place, New Delhi 110 019*

In the Netherlands: Please write to *Penguin Books Netherlands bv, Postbus 3507, NL-1001 AH Amsterdam*

In Germany: Please write to *Penguin Books Deutschland GmbH, Metzlerstrasse 26, 60594 Frankfurt am Main*

In Spain: Please write to *Penguin Books S. A., Bravo Murillo 19, 1° B, 28015 Madrid*

In Italy: Please write to *Penguin Italia s.r.l., Via Felice Casati 20, I–20124 Milano*

In France: Please write to *Penguin France S. A., 17 rue Lejeune, F–31000 Toulouse*

In Japan: Please write to *Penguin Books Japan, Ishikiribashi Building, 2–5–4, Suido, Bunkyo-ku, Tokyo 112*

In South Africa: Please write to *Longman Penguin Southern Africa (Pty) Ltd, Private Bag X08, Bertsham 2013*